ALIEN HEART

Kartar Singh Duggal is one of our leading writers who writes with equal felicity in Punjabi, Urdu, Hindi and English. His writings have won several literary awards. A senior civil servant, he was the recipient of the Padma Bhushan in 1988. At present, he is the Deputy Editor-in-chief of Lotus, an organ of the Afro-Asian Writer's association.

This present novel, *Man Pardesi* was awarded the Punjab Government's Award for fiction in 1983.

The novel was translated from Punjabi, by Jai Ratan in close collaboration with the author.

A retired executive, Jai Ratan is a founder-member of the Writer's Workshop, Calcutta. Besides writing in English, he has translated from Hindi, Urdu and Punjabi. His translations include the works of Krishan Chander, Premchand, Mohan Rakesh and other Sahitya Akademi Award winners such as Amrita Pritam, Bhisham Sahni, Rajinder Singh Bedi. His work is regularly featured in English magazines. A volume of Bedi's Short Stories translated by him will shortly be published by the Sahitya Akademi.

Alien Heart

K.S. Duggal
Translated by Jai Ratan

DISHA BOOKS

ALIEN HEART

Disha Books

Registered Office
3-6-272 Himayatnagar, Hyderabad 500 029

Other Offices
Kamani Marg, Ballard Estate, Bombay 400 038
17 Chittaranjan Avenue, Calcutta 700 072
160 Anna Salai, Madras 600 002
1/24 Asaf Ali Road, New Delhi 110 002
80/1 Mahatma Gandhi Road, Bangalore 560 001
3-6-272 Himayatnagar, Hyderabad 500 029
Birla Mandir Road, Patna 800 004
S.C. Goswami Road, Panbazar, Guwahati 781 001
'Patiala House', 16-A Ashok Marg, Lucknow 226 001

© Orient Longman 1990
ISBN 0 86131 997 4

Published by
Orient Longman Limited
1/24 Asaf Ali Road
New Delhi 110 002

Phototypeset by
Jaygee Enterprises
4th Floor
Kamala Arcade
669 Anna Salai
Madras 600 006

Printed in India at
Nu Tech Photolithographers
10/1 & 2-B Jhilmil Industrial Area
Shahdara, Delhi 110 032

*To Qusm Khemani
whom I had promised another work*

1

"My husband! My master! Tell me what am I to do? Where shall I go?"

It was the heart-rending cry of a woman. The *mujawar* of the graveyard looked around in surprise. A woman in the graveyard at this late hour of evening ! He could not believe his ears. Darkness was spreading and the trees standing stiffly erect had lost their shadows. It was always like this in winter; in the twinkling of an eye the night would come down, blotting out the evening. The mujawar looked up. It was a moonless night.

"Karamdin, stop dreaming!" The mujawar pulled himself up and sat down facing the west by the side of his *pir's* grave to say his evening *namaz*. Even in daytime his *hujra* remained dark as night. He sat there, his back towards the rows of graves.

This graveyard, dotted with graves covered with brick and mortar, was a preserve of the rich of the city. For the past few months the city had seen much lawlessness and turmoil, and almost every day a bier made its way to the graveyard. Since the outbreak of communal trouble not a day passed when one or two dead bodies were not brought for burial. The mujawar would get tired reciting the *durud* before the dead were lowered into their graves. It appeared as if Doomsday was at hand.

"People say our country has won freedom," the mujawar muttered to himself. It is freedom to knife one another, freedom to ransack houses or freedom to burn and loot, freedom to molest women!"

He continued muttering "May God have mercy on us! Only yesterday the radio was blaring: 'Mahatma Gandhi has brought freedom to the country without shedding a drop of blood. He has done it peacefully, nonviolently. The whole range of human history cannot show another example of such glorious achievement.' What blatant lies! These radio people can deceive the world but not the mujawar of this graveyard. How can they hide facts from him? He saw graves being dug day and night to receive the dead. He found the graveyard always crowded with mourners.

The mujawar, it seemed, was turning into a cynic. "I propose that these graves made of brick and mortar be levelled down to make room for others," he said to himself. The Holy Prophet had said that we should build *kutcha* graves so that these are wiped out in due course, leaving no trace behind. Who knows we may have to do this out of sheer necessity? If this terrible game of stabbing one another continues in the city at the present rate, if the Muslim plunges his knife into the Hindu's body and the Hindu flies at the Muslim's throat, then independent India and independent Pakistan will both soon become a vast graveyard. We never before had heard of neighbours killing neighbours. Can there be a greater sacrilege than that? Earlier, when a bier was brought to the graveyard the procession of mourners was made up of Muslims and Hindus almost in equal number. But today you won't find a single tufted fellow among the Muslims.

"Surely, the world is coming to an end. When brother has no regard for brother — what else is a neighbour if not a brother? — you can be sure that Doomsday has arrived. Doomsday is no different from this. So did my mentor say, my blue-robed pir. May God bless him! He made no difference between Hindus and Muslims; he treated both in the same way. That was why Hindus made offerings at his shrine and Sikhs bowed their heads before it. And now, ever since the cry of Pakistan has gone up, no Hindu or Sikh ventures here. Let Pakistan be what it wants to be. We have nothing to do with it. It belongs to the Pakistanis. Can one desert one's country, one's home? Others may leave their homes, but not I. I can't forsake my graveyard. How can I?"

Though the mujawar was saying his namaz all this while, his mind was roving without his knowing it. It was still preoccupied with these thoughts when his prayers came to an end. "A curse on such vile thoughts!" – the mujawar reproved himself, as he came out of his hujra. He had gone through his namaz without his mind having engaged in it at all.

That was precisely what Guru Nanak, who was regarded as their *guru* by Hindus and as their pir by Muslims, had said to the *maulvi* of Sultanpur: "How could I join you for namaz? You were apparently saying your prayers but all the while your mind was on the colt you had left loose in your courtyard." "In that case you could have ignored the maulvi and joined me," said the nawab of Sultanpur. "But you were not present either," Baba Nanak retorted, "You were buying horses in Kabul."

"Karamdin, you are also like the nawab," the mujawar scolded himself. "Your kneeling down and bowing so many times are nothing but sham, an eyewash. Just look at that woman prostrating herself over that grave, as if she is going to gather up the entire grave in her arms. See how she has wrapped herself in a sheet of white cloth. White is a symbol of purity and simplicity. That's the way one should pray. From her bearing she appears to be from a sheikh's family. Oh yes, the sheikhs have their graves laid out in that corner of the graveyard. All of these are made of brick and mortar, with marble tablets on which inscriptions are carved. Now she is crying! What an anguished cry! She must be under great mental suffering, the way she beats her head against the grave. It must be her husband's."

She cried: "My husband! My master! I feel so forlorn, so helpless."

Darkness was coming down over the graveyard. The place looked so bleak and forsaken that a tremor went through the woman's heart. This was no time for a woman to stir out alone. She may have thought that she would ask the mujawar to escort her home. Evil days. No woman dared go out alone. Perhaps life held no attraction for her any more and death no terror. For all she cared, let some Hindu raise the cry of 'Har Har Mahadev!' and throw an acid bomb on her. Let a Sikh kill her at one stroke with his *kirpan*. Perhaps she was no more enamoured of life. Perhaps she had come to wail at her husband's grave in the hope of getting some mental relief. But nothing of the sort seemed to have happened. The fire of grief was still raging in her heart. She felt as if somebody had ripped through a part of her body with a sharp weapon, as if the warp and woof of her life had got tangled and she lay prostrate in utter helplessness.

As she approached the hujra the ground seemed to move under the mujawar's feet. She was no other than Begum Haseeb, the great sheikh's wife! May God give peace to his soul! He had been called to his eternal rest many years ago. He was a God-fearing man, meticulous about his prayers and fasts, and was held in high esteem by all. The very mention of his name showed a path to the people . He was a great patriot and there was no love lost between him and the British rulers. Even so, the *tehsildar* and the police inspector deferred to him and the British Collector called at his bungalow. Once his begum's photograph had appeared in the newspaper in which she was sitting alongside the Collector's wife. Many eyebrows had gone up. The orthodox Muslims had said that a

Alien Heart

Muslim woman living in *purdah* had no business to expose herself to public gaze in the company of a *feringi* woman. But Begum Haseeb did not care. She had accompanied her husband, a renowned political leader, on his trips to far-off places such as Peshawar, Lahore, Delhi and Calcutta. Some said that even the Britishers were scared of him. More so because he was a reputed lawyer. It was said that his client never lost case in court, thanks to the sheikh's knowledge of law. He used to live in a big bungalow on a large plot of land in an exclusive part of the city where high government officials and other elite of the city lived.

Begum Haseeb's voice had gone hoarse with crying. She tried to speak to the mujawar but her voice died in her throat. Then the mujawar understood and said, "Bismillah! Bismillah! Begum Sahiba, I'll come with you to your house. It's too late to go out alone these days."

Karamdin quickly thrust his feet into his ragged slippers and started for the Begum's house. Before leaving he picked up his staff, which was resting against the wall in a corner of the verandah. The staff had been given to him by his pir. While going out he made it a point to arm himself with the ancient staff. He had great faith in it. It would ward off any evil-doer, be he a Hindu, a Sikh or anyone else.

"We are living in bad times," the mujawar said, as he walked alongside the Begum. Bad times, indeed. Not long ago Hindus used to offer cloth-lengths at my pir's shrine and Sikhs came to show their respect here. No one returned disappointed. Their wishes were always fulfilled. The Hindu and the Sikh devotees, in fact, outnumbered the Muslims. But for the past many months I have not seen even a single Hindu or Sikh visiting this shrine. Not even by mistake do their feet stray in this direction. Sometimes I wonder how they manage these days. What do they do to mend broken strands of their lives? In whom do they repose trust? Where do they seek solace?

"I'm talking of the days when they were indiscriminately arresting people in Punjab. That was many years ago. I haven't breathed a word about it to anybody till now. Two Sikhs had sneaked into our graveyard and hid themselves in my hujra. They loosened their hair and tossed it over their backs. They would grind *bhang* twice a day for drinking and offer it to me also. I taught them to say namaz. It was the month of *Ramzan*. Like me they observed fasts and ate only in the evening. They stayed with me for six weeks. I did not reveal their presence to anybody. Many times the police came following their trail. But they went away after asking a few casual questions. I told everyone that they were mujawars of a pir's shrine from the Frontier. They were jovial men. Self-sacrificing and daring. They carried their lives on the palms of their hands. They would not have hesitated if it came to dying in the cause of their country. All the time they said that they would throw the feringis out of the country for they were the cause of all discord between the Hindus and the Muslims. Hindustanis were all *bhai-bhai* they insisted."

The mujawar was talking in this vein when Begum Haseeb stumbled and fell down on the path.

2

Seema, Begum Haseeb's charming young daughter, had married a Sikh youth. This had shaken the Begum very badly. When she got the telegram which conveyed the

Alien Heart

news, tears ran from her eyes in torrents and she writhed like a tormented fish. It was a shock for her especially because she was a widow, and she did not know what to do about it.

Her husband had died several years ago. A man of some eminence, he was known all over the country and commanded great respect. While he lived, Begum Haseeb did not have a care in the world. Then the irreversible happened. He was quite hale and hearty all day. In the evening he had a stroke and at night he was gone. As time passed, the Begum reconciled herself to the new situation. "Qudsia, you have a son and two daughters," she consoled herself. "They are full of promise and are sure to do well in life. You lack nothing. You should be grateful to God and abide by his wishes." She accepted her lot without bitterness, thinking that that was how Allah had willed it. A mother of three children, her youth had long since declined. Yet there was not a trace of grey in her hair. On the other hand, the grace and mellowness of middle age had lent a peculiar charm to her presence.

And now in just one day she had become pale and weak, haggard as if all strength had ebbed away from her body. Seema's news came as a severe blow to her. She collapsed on the divan as she read the telegram. Fortunately, her younger daughter Zeba, who was about to leave for school, saw her mother collapse and immediately took charge of her. She called for Dr. Gopal from across the road. The doctor gave her mother an injection, followed by one more which revived the Begum.

Zeba felt bitter about her sister. As she returned after seeing Dr. Gopal off at the gate, she muttered to herself, "If Seema wanted to demean herself, she should have married a Hindu. That would not have been so bad." But how could she have eloped with a Hindu when she was in love with a Sikh? Zeba asked herself. The taste in her mouth turned sour. "There's a time for everything," she grumbled. "This is no time for a Muslim girl to marry a non-Muslim. And a Sikh at that! *Toba,* what sacrilege!" Although Zeba was still studying in school, she seemed to be wise beyond her years. She came back into the house, her mind still full of thoughts of her sister. Her mother it seemed, had fallen asleep. She was lying in bed with her eyes closed.

But Begum Haseeb was not sleeping. She was just feigning sleep for she did not have the courage to face her younger daughter. Zeba was already doomed. What prospects of marriage could she have, as the younger sister of a girl who had brought shame to her family. Would any young man agree to marry her? The Begum just could not believe that a girl could ignore her own religion and defame herself for the sake of a Sikh classfellow. Specially these days when Sikhs had become anathema. They had ransacked village after Muslim village in East Punjab and slaughtered all the inhabitants. They had butchered train-loads of Muslims on their way to Pakistan and molested their women. Trains dripping with blood had gone across the border to the other side. Master Tara Singh had challenged the Muslims at Lahore by waving his sword. Word had reached Begum Haseeb that the Babbar Akalis had gone berserk and were combing the countryside in search of Muslims. They even smelled out Muslims from their hideouts and hacked them to pieces gleefully. Not only in Punjab, they had even started such carnage in Delhi.

Under such conditions it was unimaginable that a Muslim girl could marry a Sikh youth. An act that was taboo even in normal times, it would never be excused in these days of upheaval. Begum Haseeb cursed herself silently for not having acted on the advice of her Pakistani relatives. Long before the partition her husband's brother now living in Pakistan had frantically asked her to move to West Punjab. Just a few days before partition her husband's sister had come to fetch her from Lahore.

"Does one ever abandon one's own country?" Begum Haseeb gave just one cryptic reply to all of them. Her son was studying medicine in London. He was not prepared to adopt Pakistani citizenship. Her husband's younger brother was an engineer at Lahore. He pleaded with Begum Haseeb to shift to Lahore at least temporarily till the storm blew over. But she would not agree, "What if the Boundary Commission awards Lahore to India?" she asked.

The Boundary Commission announced its award. Lahore became a part of Pakistan. From every nook and corner of Pakistan Sikhs and Hindus were uprooted and chased out to India. Those that remained behind were massacred to clean Pakistan of infidels and make it pure in every respect. The people there now all belonged to Islam, there being not one who did not profess the faith. Except of course of a small number of Christians. But they had affinity with Muslims for like Muslims they also swore by their holy book. Besides, they professed the faith of feringis. It was feringis who had had a big hand in carving out Pakistan for the Muslims. Otherwise, the Hindus were ready to gobble up the whole of Hindustan. It was said, "Gandhi is very cunning. A Hindu bigot at heart. He had the evil design of making Hindus rule over Muslims forgetting that Muslims had ruled over Hindus for centuries."

Had Seema been living in Delhi then, they would have tried to make her see reason and got her to change her mind. But how could they go to Amritsar at a time when every life was in danger. In Punjab murderous assaults had become a routine matter. It had been converted into a veritable slaughter-house. While Sikhs and Hindus were being wiped out in West Pakistan, in East Punjab they were playing with the lives of Muslims. No Muslim could be so foolhardy as to venture into Amritsar. Muslims travelling by train were singled out and killed brutally. Nobody could tell how Seema managed to reach Amritsar. It would have been better if she had been killed on the way. That would have spared the family all this humiliation. Thousands of Muslim girls had preferred to die rather than fall into the clutches of these fiends. Seema could also have joined those glorious dead.

"I won't live in this country any longer," Begum Haseeb told herself. "I don't care for my property, nor for relatives living here. They can go to hell for all I care. For that matter I have relatives in Pakistan too. And it is never too late to form new links if it comes to that. One daughter has let me down and I cannot be sure of what the other wants. It is a blessing to be born into Islam. How can one be so stupid as to forego such a boon? When my sister-in-law Ismet came from Lahore to fetch me, I should have gone with her. I was foolish to miss such a glorious opportunity. But how could I have gone? Both my daughters were studying here. Seema in college and Zeba in school. Yes, how could I go leaving such a big bungalow behind? And all those shops which fetch such high rents? My sisters, my brothers? The entire city knows me. In every lane they are familiar with the name of Qudsia Begum. The whole neighbourhood dotes on me. We have our family graveyard here where my husband lies in eternal sleep. And so also my father-in-law. In the last election I voted for the Congress. I had marked my ballot in the name of Mahatma Gandhi and had asked others to do likewise. Then I started learning Hindi at my age and persuaded my children to learn this language. I told them that if one has to make friends with neighbours one must learn their language.

"But now I'll not live in this country – Hindu, Hindi, Hindustan!"

Alien Heart

3

"My dear Ammi!" – a few days later there was a letter from Seema. "You must have received my telegram," she had written. "I can imagine how terribly shocked you must be on learning that I have married Inder Mohan. The whole household must have been upset and all of you must be cursing me for what I have done. I am conscious of the fact that I am as good as dead for you. I have no place in your house. You would not even like to look at my face. My brother and sister will discard me. I have been thrown very far from them. But I am ready to pay the price, however high, for the decision I have taken.

"I fear that you may even burn this letter without reading it through to the end. But I have only one desire – a last desire of a daughter. You must read this letter to its very last line and only then make up your mind. In that case I will have no grudge against you.

"You know Inder Mohan, of course. He visited our house once and stayed for the night. Then he was studying with me at college. That we were fond of each other and moved about together was no secret. Everybody in our college said that we were made for each other and could marry any day, although there was no truth in it.

"I felt great sympathy for Inder. His family had lost everything in Pakistan. His village was sacked and his parents killed. Miscreants had carried away his young sister and there has been no trace of her since then. Although Inder has never said this to me in so many words, but it seems I remind him of his sister. Perhaps you will recall my having told you once that Inder's sister's name was also Seema. Maybe that was why I struck a soft chord in his heart.

"In India it is easy to establish the relationship of brother and sister, and so many people do it without attaching any meaning to it. But ours was a different case. We were friends and devoted to each other. As far as possible we spent our evenings together. I did not find anything odd about this. I am Sheikh Haseeb's daughter, am I not? My Abba made no distinction between a Hindu and a Muslim, a Sikh and a Christian.

"You will remember that Abba had the first taste of jail in Nabha. He was jailed in connection with a movement launched by the Sikhs. He rotted in the feringi jail for many months in supporting the cause of his Punjabi countrymen. They were the same Punjabis who had received the feringis' bullets on their chests at Jallianwalla Bagh. This was the sacred place where Hindus, Sikhs and Muslims had gathered to defy the might of the British rulers. Their blood had mingled down the drains of Amritsar.

"As you know, like a true Muslim Abba was very particular about his namaz. Yet all his life he stood by the Congress and fought for the country's freedom and did his best to promote Hindu-Muslim unity. I can never forget that I am the daughter of Sheikh Haseeb. Of course, there were occasions when he did not agree with the Congress and was even called a communalist. But he never let down the Mahatma. When there is more than one vessel on a tray, one vessel is bound to strike another. Misunderstandings are bound to happen. But Abba remained loyal to his country till the very end. He died with the slogan of *'Inqilab zindabad!'* on his lips.

"Ammi, I shall never forget Abba's funeral procession. Thousands of Hindus accompanied it and shed tears at his untimely death. And there were Sikhs too who put their shoulders to his bier. Even though the Muslims objected, his body was wrapped in the tri-colour. The

Alien Heart

citizens of Meerut, Hindus, Sikhs and Muslims alike, insisted on doing him this last honour.

"Ammi, I am the daughter of that exalted Abba and my main purpose in writing to you is to tell you about the kind of husband I have chosen for myself the man who is going to be my life-companion. The daughter of a worthy father, I want to be the wife of a worthy husband.

"I am sure you remember Inder's visit to Meerut. He had stayed with us for the night. The next day we were going to Delhi by the evening train. We had just got into an empty compartment when half a dozen young men barged in there. Apparently college boys, they looked a decent lot and spoke English. The train had just started when two of them pounced upon Inder and started beating him. The rest of the boys fell upon me, shouting 'Pakistan Zindabad!' One of them pinched my cheek and another tugged at my hair. But that was just the beginning. They tried to undress me and, failing to pull off my clothes, just tore away what they could. I was appalled at their behaviour. They were worse than beasts. They even tried to rape me.

"I told them again and again that I was a Muslim. I told them Abba's name but they didn't listen to what I was saying. They threatened me that if I raised any alarm they would kill my Sikh companion also along with me. All the way from Meerut to Delhi they struck blows at Inder and hurt him in other ways. They pulled out scissors and clipped his long hair. So did they cut off mine in the name of Pakistan. When the train slowed down near Delhi they jumped off. While going away they also tore away the locket from my neck, the one you had given me on my last birthday.

"I covered myself with whatever clothes were left on my body. We were feeling too embarrassed to look at each other. We did not know what to do. The dark night outside only added to our confusion. We were afraid that those *goondas* may invade our compartment again, so we locked the door from inside.

"The story does not end there. After reaching Delhi we did not go to our hostels but spent the night together in a hotel. All the time Inder kept cursing himself for having accompanied me. He said I had to face this horror because of his being a Sikh. Also the alarm chain was not working on the train. He had pulled at it repeatedly without any result.

"Ammi, today I am the same Inder's wife. I have a lot more to tell you. But I don't want to miss the post and shall stop here for the present.... Your daughter, Seema."

4

Begum Haseeb had just finished reading Seema's letter when her husband's elder brother Sheikh Shabbir came into the room. He looked frantic. He had just got the news. Begum Haseeb hid the letter under her pillow. Her brother-in-law, a landlord, was a man of very orthodox and old-fashioned views and rabidly communal-minded.

"I have been telling you all this time that there is no need to educate girls. And now you can see for yourself what disaster this girl has brought to us. You remember how head-strong and self-willed your husband was. He deluded himself all his life and held on to strings dangled by Hindus. Hindu-Muslim unity is nonsense. Now you can eat the fruits of your friendship with Hindus and

Alien Heart

Sikhs. This girl of yours was always suspect in my eyes. I never liked her ways. In the first place, tell me why you had to send her to Delhi for studies? Do the girls of all other families go to Delhi for their education? And what a lame excuse she made up saying that the subject she wanted to study was not taught here. Now you know the kind of subject she had gone to study!"

There was no stopping Sheikh Shabbir. "Had she been my daughter, I would have shot her dead," he continued. "Don't worry, I'm not going to forgive her anyway. And to avenge the honour and prestige of our family I'll make sure that that Sikh scoundrel also suffers. He must be having a sister. I'll have her abducted. And if he has a mother I'll not spare her either. Even if I have to spend thousands of rupees to accomplish my task. The goondas of our city carry on their dirty work as far as Bombay and Calcutta. They are in my pay. They know their job, for they have been at this game for more than a year. They have molested scores of Hindu and Sikh girls. Those characterless girls accept it without even a whimper. Hindu religion is no religion. It's just another name for a garbage bin which holds all sorts of rubbish. And my boys have cut off the long hair of scores of Sikh boys and girls. Teach them a lesson.

"I say your husband was to blame for it. He started it by having Mahatma Gandhi as his mentor. Why don't you ask Mahatma Gandhi now to come to the rescue of your loving daughter? Ask him to rescue her from that Sikh brute. Oh, the way he used to brag about Hindu-Muslim unity! When Jawaharlal's sister Vijayalakshmi wanted to marry Dr. Mahmood, he put his foot down. He was dead against this marriage. Why? Wouldn't that have promoted Hindu-Muslim unity? If a Muslim girl can marry a Hindu, why can't a Hindu girl marry a Muslim boy? Yes, tell me, why not?"

Begum Haseeb's elder sister-in-law came into the room, beating her forehead. She started wailing and pulled at her hair as if she was lamenting over somebody's death. She punctuated her wailing with abuses aimed at Seema. Seeing her, Begum Haseeb could not hold back her tears. She also started crying. Her sister-in-law clung to her and wailed all the louder. The whole house seemed to be in turmoil, bringing all the maidservants outside the Begum's room to watch. Zeba came in and stood in a corner, shedding tears.

Then it was the neighbours' turn. They came in a swarm. And so did the distant relatives. The whole house seemed to have gone into mourning. Begum Haseeb sat there, feeling at a loss as to how to cope with the situation. For the first time no Hindu friend had turned up to lighten the burden of her sorrow. Nor had any Sikh come. Those who came were all Muslims, most of them good neighbours and the others relatives and family friends. They sat in the main room in small groups, whispering among themselves and making all sorts of conjectures.

"The girl was abducted from this very room."

"They were Hindu and Sikh goondas. The women were alone in the house. They pulled out daggers to threaten the girl and drove off with her in a car."

"No, she went with them willingly. She was a party to this game. She had clandestine relations with the boy. The mother would not allow it. But the girl did not care. She just ignored her mother."

"She was only waiting for a chance. While going she made a clean sweep of all the jewellery in the house."

"And now she is entrenched at Amritsar. A clever girl, indeed. No Muslim can venture there."

"You are right. For a Muslim to go to Amritsar would mean certain death. We dare not even look in that direction."

Then they went into a kind of conference. At the instance of Sheikh Haseeb's elder brother it was decided. that they should lodge a complaint with the police to the effect that Hindu and Sikh goondas had abducted a Muslim girl from her house. They had also looted all the jewellery in the house. It was decided that a small delegation should go to Delhi. One never knew, such a move may produce results. Many of Sheikh Haseeb's friends were now holding high positions in the Congress government. Jawaharlal Nehru himself knew the Sheikh.

Begum Haseeb sat there with no expression on her face. Nothing seemed to be registering on her mind. Only dark circles seemed to be forming before her eyes. She felt as if she was going down a deep well. After a while her head fell over her shoulder with a jerk and she fainted. The women present there crowded around her. Some rubbed her palms and others sprinkled water over her face, while still others ran out to fetch a doctor.

When Begum Haseeb came to after some time and opened her eyes she found Dr. Saleem sitting by her bedside and not Dr. Gopal. Dr. Gopal had his clinic just across the road and he was their family physician. He had called here just the other day. But now, being a Hindu, he had become a stranger to them. Dr. Saleem had come from three kilometres away. A Muslim doctor alone must attend to a Muslim patient!

Begum Haseeb looked around for her servant, Kalu, but he was nowhere to be seen. He was their family servant. His mother had also served the family and his father had died while working here. Kalu had been brought up like a member of this household and played with the children of the family. Sheikh Saheb had even tried to send him to school but it was not in Kalu's lot to learn to read and write. He ended up as a domestic like his father. Kalu used to follow the Begum like a shadow, specially since the communal trouble had started. At night he would place his cot on the verandah and sleep there. Nobody ventured near their house. He had a fierce-looking watchdog as his companion.

Then Zeba hurried in, panting. "There's a *tonga* standing behind our house," she whispered into her mother's ear. "Kalu has put his luggage in the tonga. I think he is leaving us for good. Dubboo, our dog, is also going with him."

Begum Haseeb quickly got down from her bed and followed out of the room.

"This woman will never learn," a relative said.

"A woman's wisdom gets buried under her heel," another jibed.

"Considering the times we are passing through, can a Hindu servant stay with a Muslim family?"

"I won't be surprised if this fellow Kalu had a hand in spoiling the girl."

"Don't worry, I'll set a few goondas after him. They will take good care of him."

"This family itself is responsible for bringing about its own ruin. They have been indulging in all sorts of absurd ideas."

"Hindu-Muslim friendship now makes no sense. We have carved out Pakistan for ourselves. Now as advised by our Qaid-e-Azam the next step will be to connect Punjab with Bengal."

"We shall have to make many more sacrifices, specially those of us who live in UP. Our task is still incomplete."

"We have ruled over this land for centuries. Insha Allah, the flag of the crescent will once again fly over the whole subcontinent."

"We must now try to save the other girl. Find a good Muslim young man and be done with her."

"If a young man is not around, a middle-aged man would do. Even a widower should serve the purpose. But marry she must."

"Even if the man had a wife living with him, it should make no difference. Islam allows four wives. What I mean is that the girl should have a roof over her head. The sooner the better. A young girl is a great responsibility."

"Specially girls with no male member in the family can be very vulnerable."

Begum Haseeb returned barefoot. She was weeping. Zeba, coming close behind, was also sobbing. Kalu had refused to listen to them. At their insistence he had relented only to the extent of leaving Dubboo behind.

5

People called on Begum Haseeb, looking solemn as if it were a house of mourning and they had come to condole with her. The visits were like a deluge in which Seema's letter was lost like a piece of straw. The Muslims had drawn nearer to one another. It was all so unforeseen that Begum Haseeb was taken utterly by surprise. All the visitors vehemently disparaged their Hindu neighbours and everyone of them had some outlandish plan or the other up his sleeve. Many were in the process of migrating to Pakistan, while quite a few were toying with the idea of doing so. There were many families where the younger members had gone across the border, while their old parents were biding their time in India. It was not uncommon for brothers and sisters to have been separated, the sisters being married in India and the brothers holding jobs in Pakistan.

Surprises rained upon the Begum. Everybody had his own story to tell. Some had been forced to stay behind because of their property and others because of their business which they could not give up so easily. Some were tied to permanent jobs so that while their bodies remained in India their hearts had gone to Pakistan. At times Begum Haseeb felt that her husband perhaps had been deluding himself all his life. He had been building a house of cards and the structure had collapsed at one blow.

There was news about Kashmir which the Begum read with avid interest. Pakistani tribals had invaded the valley and the Kashmiri Muslims, Hindus and Sikhs were resisting the invaders with grim determination. There was also disquieting news from the eastern part of the country. Mahatma Gandhi had been trudging from one place to another in Noakhali district, putting the rioters to shame for their misdeeds. The members of the minority community were being rehabilitated in their villages, besides given other assistance. The government was constructing new houses for those whose homes had been burnt by the rioters. Peace committees had been formed in the sensitive areas. Places of worship were being repaired and schools were being given aid to enable them to resume teaching.

That day Sheikh Abdullah had made a fighting speech at the United Nations. "Kashmir is an inalienable part of India," he had declared on the floor of the House. It was the final decision of the people of Kashmir that they had cast their lot with India. They would throw out the Pakistani invaders and clear every inch of their land of the enemy. Even Mahatma Gandhi, the apostle of nonviolence, had justified India's stand on Kashmir. This war, he said, was being fought to uphold *dharma*. It was a war against untruth, treachery, tyranny and naked brute force.

Begum Haseeb's head started reeling. She was so confused that she did not know where her sympathies lay.

Alien Heart

Thus lost in thought she wandered towards the servant quarters. The door of Kalu's room was ajar. Its window was also open. He had swept and tidied up the room before leaving. Wasn't he a Hindu, a stickler for cleanliness? There was not even a spot of dust on the floor, much less a scrap of paper. The Begum noticed this and smiled. In a corner an idol was still resting against the wall, a stick of incense and a match-box lying beside it. He had not taken the idol away with him. Then it occurred to the Begum that Hindus generally hesitated to remove an image from where it is once installed. She suddenly felt moved at the sight of the idol. Without thinking about it, she sat down on the ground, struck a match and, lighting a stick of incense placed it in front of the idol. She did it in the way she had seen Kalu do it.

In the rising smoke of the incense the Begum went down memory lane. Kalu was born in this very room. His father had brought the good news, almost dancing in joy. They had come to see the new-born child. The infant looked like a leech, so thin and shrivelled he was. Perhaps he was prematurely born. But Sheikh Saheb made sure that the child was properly cared for and saved it from what looked like certain death. Kalu was brought up with the other children of the family and grew into a healthy lad. "I'm fifteen days older than you," he would tease Seema. "You must call me Bhaijan." He was deeply devoted to the family. He took such a care of the house that not one dared touch even a blade of its grass. He would invariably switch off the light if there was nobody in room and turn off the tap, so that there should be no waste of water. The fans, too, must be switched off every time one went out of a room. During the days of rioting he mixed easily with the Hindus and also befriended the Muslims. He had the knack of being present at every trouble spot. "There's one great advantage in my being named Kalu," he would say. "Hindus think I'm a Hindu, while Muslims take me for a Muslim."

"But what is the truth?" once Begum Haseeb had asked him.

"I'm neither a Hindu nor a Muslim," he had replied parrot-like. "I was born to Hindu parents and brought up by a Muslim family. So I'm neither a Hindu nor a Muslim. I am just a man."

While returning from Kalu's room the Begum recalled that Seema had promised to write her again. Several days had passed and still she had not heard from her. In these unsettled times the postal system did not always work. Miscreants could stop a train anywhere. They could plunge a knife into a postman's back in any lane.

Begum Haseeb had just returned to her room when her husband's elder brother again came charging into her room. "Bibi, you should drown yourself in a fist full of water!" he exclaimed. He was holding an Urdu newspaper in his hand which he flung towards his sister-in-law. His face had turned red with rage. What calamity had befallen the family. She picked up the newspaper from the floor and ran her eyes over the sheet without being able to concentrate on what met her eyes. The newspaper was some local communal rag.

"This girl has really defamed us. If she wanted to marry a Sikh... well, who could stop her from doing so? But where was the need for *Anand Karaj*? They could just as well have undergone a civil marriage in the court. When her ardour had cooled and she saw these Sikhs in their true colours, she could have returned to her home. It would have been easy enough to make an application before the court and seek a divorce. But this wicked girl has left no way for return. She submitted herself to Anand Karaj. The glorious deeds of this favourite daughter of Sheikh Haseeb have been set out in this

Alien Heart

newspaper. The whole story! Her father went to *Haj* four times and now the daughter has kicked the path of her forefathers and gone her own sweet way. We can't even show our faces to the people.

"As for me, I don't think I can stay in this city any longer. How can I go to the mosque to say namaz? Today is Friday and I can't even stand in the congregation to bow my head before Allah along with the others! Toba! Toba! I didn't know we were bringing up a poisonous snake in our midst. She should have at least shown some regard for her Abba and her illustrious family. She should have shown some consideration for her younger sister who is growing like a creeper every day, waiting to be married off. Which respectable family is going to accept her now? The newspaper has spattered us with mud. Sheikh Haseeb used to advocate Hindu-Muslim unity. All his life he served as a stooge of the Mahatma and flirted with the Congress. And now his daughter has fulfilled her father's dream by marrying a Sikh.

"I called on our family lawyer on my way to your house. The government has announced an ordinance. Any change of religion and all marriages contracted under duress during the riots will have no legal sanction behind them. Such marriages will be declared null and void. All those Muslim girls who have been abducted will be restored to their families. We have only to put in an application. The police will swing into action, hunt out the girl and take her under its charge. I'm not Sheikh Sharif's son if I do not bring your daughter home within four days. Our lawyer thinks that the moment we submit our application the government will order the police to take action. If it is necessary to bribe somebody I'll not hesitate. I'll myself go with the police to Amritsar. My only fear is that bastard of a Sikh may hide the girl somewhere. I've heard that when they hear that the police is about to carry out a raid, it is a common practice to move the abducted girls to some unknown place. I know it will be difficult but if one makes a serious attempt even the impossible can become possible."

"Bhaijan, you will not have to take the trouble of searching for Seema," Begum Haseeb said after listening to her brother-in-law's harangue. "Here is Seema's letter. Just read it."

"Seema's letter?" Sheikh Shabbir looked at the Begum in amazement. He snatched the letter from her and started reading it. His face began losing colour as he quickly went through the letter. The letter finished, he sank into the sofa in a corner of the room.

"Ammi! Ammijan! Zeba came rushing in.

"Just now I saw a stick of incense burning in front of the idol in Kalu's room. He has been away for many days. The incense gets lit on its own every morning. All the servants have assembled in his room to see the miracle. Even the neighbours have started coming – Oh, Uncle, I didn't see you! I beg your pardon."

Sitting in the sofa Sheikh Shabbir was still poring over Seema's letter.

6

Sheikh Shabbir remained engrossed in reading Seema's letter. After a while, when Begum Haseeb looked up again, she saw that the letter had dropped from his hand, his mouth had fallen open and a ghastly expression had come over his face. "Bhaijan, Bhaijan, is something the matter with you?" she cried. Zeba had left the room.

Alien Heart

Sheikh Shabbir was an affluent Muslim of the city. He owned a lot of land and lived in a big ancestral *haveli*. His assets ran into lakhs and he was regarded as the leader of the local Muslim community. To uphold his prestige he was ever ready to help others and had the knack of pleasing everyone. He professed loyalty to the Congress and also lauded the communalists whom he helped financially. The politicians on either side did not bother about where the money was coming from so long it kept coming. Sheikh Shabbir doled out thousands of rupees to the Congress and in equal measure to communal parties such as the Muslim League. All had a good word for him and they regarded him as an enlightened and well-meaning money-bag. But ever since the communal trouble had started, he had begun to patronise the trouble-makers. He gave them money, he gave them arms. And if it came to that he did not mind hiding the miscreants in his fortress-like haveli.

The Muslim goondas who had attacked Seema and Inder Mohan were actually in the pay of Sheikh Shabbir. They were from among those to whom he had been giving money for some time past. He had even bought for them country-made revolvers. He clearly remembered now that they had come to him and narrated to him the whole story with great gusto. As proof, they had also given him that locket which he must have carefully put away in a safe place.

"Today we did it with a Sikh girl," they had boastfully reported to Sheikh Shabbir. "I planned the whole thing," one of them said. "It was my idea to pounce upon her Sikh brother first." At this his companion chipped in and said that if he had not slapped her, she would not have been tamed. No, she stopped shouting only when he put the point of his dagger at her bosom, a third goonda said, trying to take away the credit from the other two. "I am a Muslim girl," she had kept crying. She had also mumbled her father's name which they could not quite catch. But they were quite convinced that she was a Sikh girl. Her hairdo was like that of a Panjabi girl and so was the swell of her bosom. And her wheatish complexion too. All these were pointers to her being a Panjabi girl. Also she was tall and strong and could have easily floored each of them individually. But she was one against six. At first she fought against them with the fury of a lioness. She scratched their faces with her nails and dug her teeth into their flesh. Only when she seemed to have got tired and unable to hold out any longer she gave in. Or perhaps she was on the verge of passing out and could do nothing but submit to them. They clipped her hair, the long hair of a Sikh girl, lock by lock.

"No, no, no!" Sheikh Shabbir suddenly plucked at his hair with both hands and ran out of the room.

"Bhaijan, Bhaijan!" the Begum shouted and followed him upto the gate. But Sheikh Shabbir kept muttering something without stopping to look back at the Begum. She returned to her house wringing her hands. When she entered her room, she saw Zeba reading the letter which her uncle had dropped on the floor while rushing out. After finishing the letter, Zeba kept it with herself. Later on the Begum did not ask for it nor did Zeba part with it on her own.

That evening Begum Haseeb went to see her brother-in-law at his haveli. She had been informed on the phone that he was running a high temperature and was in delirium. He had been raving all this time. The doctor had applied an iced sponge to his forehead but that had brought him no relief. Begum Haseeb was greatly worried. This was no ordinary fever. In the morning the way he had left her house showing signs of grave mental strain suggested there was something seriously wrong with him.

As she went into his room, Sheikh Shabbir fished out Seema's locket from under his pillow and flung it at the

Alien Heart

Begum's face. "So you have come to claim your daughter's locket!" he cried. "Here, take it!" His eyes blazing fire, he again started raving. His wife, his children and the neighbours who had collected around his bed on hearing about his condition looked at each other without speaking. Then Sheikh Shabbir started crying. Gesturing to the Begum to sit on the bed by his side, he broke into hiccups till his crying changed into a wail. The doctor paid another visit and gave the Sheikh another injection. It was only in the late hours of the night that he fell asleep.

Everybody wanted to know the story behind the locket. The locket undoubtedly belonged to Seema. But nobody could explain how it had come into her uncle's possession. Even Begum Haseeb was in no position to unravel this mystery.

Leaving Sheikh Shabbir asleep, the Begum returned to her house. Another letter from Seema had arrived.

"Ammijan, I have not been able to write to you all these days," the letter read. Begum Haseeb shut the door of her room and then turned to the letter. "Before people start spreading rumours about Inder Mohan and me I should let you know the facts. I have decided to tell you the whole story as to how our marriage came about and in this Inder is in full agreement with me.

"As you know conditions in Punjab are still far from normal. Refugees are trekking in and Muslims are still migrating in an unending stream. Looting is still quite common and women are still being abducted. Even today Hindus are thirsting after their Muslim neighbours' blood. In Amritsar which is known as the Guru's holy city, I find every other man's hands dripping with blood. Every refugee who crosses the Wagah border has one or the other of his limbs missing. Many have lost their daughters and others their sons. Mothers have given their lives to shield their daughters and fathers have died trying to see their sons safely across. Those who were millionaires yesterday have become paupers today and go begging from door to door.

"Under such circumstances it was impossible for me to seek your prior consent and for you to accede to my request. I know it will break your heart to know that I have married a non-Muslim. Sitting here, I can see tears flowing from your eyes. But, Ammi, I am happy at the way things have happened. I am really happy. Perhaps this is how Allah had willed it.

"Only a few days have passed but I have already started liking the Panjabi language. It does not sound strange to me. I have already learnt how to wear salwar and kameez. I am also getting used to Punjabi food: lassi and butter, roti and saag. Nobody here seems to be fond of rice. I no longer miss it.

"Our marriage has become the talk of the town and our photograph appears frequently in newspapers. People seem to have taken a liking to us. Inder has managed to get a job and a good house to live in. They have opened a refugee camp in the Khalsa College and both of us are working there. It makes my flesh creep to hear of brutalities committed on this side of the border. The atrocities committed on Sikhs and Hindus on the other side are no less hideous. Both sides have tarnished their fair names; they are both equally to blame. But I am happy, very happy. Even though I am painfully conscious of the fact that I have been separated from you, I deem myself fortunate that I have married Inder.

"Ammi, I am looking forward to the day when I shall step into my mother's house along with Inder. In marrying a man like Inder I am sure I have Abba's tacit approval. Your daughter............Seema."

7

"But where was the need for Seema to marry a Sikh?" Zeba said sourly. She was sitting at the breakfast table with her mother.

Zeba was in a sulky mood and was talking to her mother with an edge in her voice. It was Seema's birthday and Begum Haseeb was missing her elder daughter all the more for it. She looked at Zeba's face and could see that the girl was feeling miserable. Zeba pushed away her cup of tea so violently that it crashed to the floor and broke.

"How can you be so angry even after reading her letter?" Begum Haseeb asked.

"Her letter is a big lie. It's a fraud."

"What do you mean?" her mother asked her angrily. "What nonsense are you talking?" Begum Haseeb's anger was mounting.

"If these were normal times, I would have proved to you that it is all nonsense. Seema is making a fool of us."

"Had the times been normal the poor girl would not have undergone such torture. Oh, how she must have suffered." The Begum's eyes brimmed with tears.

"The Hindus of India are responsible for this condition."

"No matter who is responsible, evil is evil."

"I still don't believe her. Her story is a sheer fabrication. It sounds like a cheap novel, a tearjerker."

Begum Haseeb gave her daughter a hard look. She was wondering whether to tell Zeba about the locket which had mysteriously come to her uncle's hand. But how did the locket come into his possession? She had been puzzling over the matter for several days. Her brother-in-law's condition was still causing anxiety and it would not be right on her part to question him at this stage.

She had just finished her breakfast when the morning mail came. There was another letter from Seema. Kalu had joined her at Amritsar. It had made her happy. "It gives me the feel of our old home," Seema had remarked.

Her letter angered Zeba all the more and she nearly started frothed at the mouth. Her lips trembled. The taste in the Begum's mouth also became bitter. Her own house had become an arena for the struggle between India and Pakistan. A wedge had been driven between members of her own family, tearing it apart. Kalu was as good as a member of her own family. They had never treated him as a mere servant. But since he was a Hindu he had forgotten his old allegiance and lost his balance. He had now gone over to live in the 'Bharat' of his own making.

"All this is Apa Seema's doing. It's a conspiracy against us. She must have poisoned Kalu's ears and tutored him to abandon us. Otherwise, could that dimwit ever have the sense to act on his own? See, how he swept his room clean before going. He had even left his Bhagwan behind." Zeba seemed to be talking to herself. "He went and quietly fetched a tonga. He put his things in the tonga and was leaving for the railway station without having a word with us. Didn't he have any regard for us? Or any sympathy? I pleaded with him and you tried to make him see sense but he never listened. If he had not known the address, how could he have gone there? And then what made him go? None of us ever gave him any cause for complaint. Why did he desert us like this? Surely, there must be some reason behind it."

Her daughter's anger set Begum Haseeb thinking. Maybe what Zeba had said had some truth in it. One could not easily take liberties with a grown-up girl in a crowded train in the short distance between Meerut and Delhi. It just did not stand to reason. True, the conditions these days were highly abnormal. But to molest a girl and beat up her male companion without any fear of consequences was like something out of an Indian film. And then for Kalu to leave them without as much as a word! It was so bewildering that Begum Haseeb could not make head or tail of it. As for Kalu, he had served them loyally all his life. He had never been impudent to her. But that day he had avoided looking at her. All the time he had kept repeating "Begum Saheb, take it that I am dead, I no longer exist for you."

She could not forget Kalu. She could overlook her own children but not Kalu. Since his going away several problems had cropped up for her. He was like a son to her, not just a servant. When Kalu was there she had never felt lonely. He would accompany her to do the daily marketing. He would collect the rent of her shops. Some litigation or the other about her property was always on and he had taken it upon himself to keep in touch with the lawyer about the court cases. He would clean the house, tend the garden and attend to a hundred other odd jobs.

Now that he was gone, street urchins had started stealing guavas from the garden. During the day the cattle roaming on the road would stray into the compound and munch at the grass, ruining the lawn. The milkman had started diluting the milk with water. He did it without fear for there was no one in the house who could pull him up for it. The gardener was absent every other day while the sweeper would just show his face and disappear within minutes after making a pretence of sweeping the floor. The old cook was still there but the food seemed to have lost its taste. When Kalu was there the table was laid on time and he did it so tastefully.

Zeba had developed a hostility against Seema. She had started hating Seema's name and spoke ill of her all the time. She complained that Seema had hung a picture of Krishna playing the flute in her bedroom. She had done it deliberately. Later Zeba discovered *bindis* in Seema's dressing table. Seema must have been wearing a bindi on her forehead while at college. She had mostly Hindu girls for friends – Vimla, Kamala, Mohini, Kalyani, Saroj and Sundari. They were too many of them to be counted. Last Ramzan she had not observed a single fast. On Eid day she was the first to go to the cinema with her Hindu girlfriend. Zeba had discovered many Hindi books in her bookcase. By and by Zeba succeeded in prejudicing her mother against Seema. Her letters came but the Begum did not care to acknowledge them. And then, her letters stopped coming. Kalu, too, seemed to have fallen from grace; by going away he had left behind a host of problems for the Begum.

Earlier she had been depending on her brother-in-law for he was a somebody in the city. But now his condition was deteriorating day by day. They had even taken him to the mental hospital at Agra for treatment. It had made no difference. Sometimes he would rail at Hindus and at others at Muslims. Sometimes he talked ill of Pakistan and at others scoffed at India. Begum Haseeb had noticed that every visit of hers was followed by a marked deterioration in his condition which was reflected in his incoherent and irrelevant talk. He had stopped coming to her house. Previously, whenever he visited her, he attended to a number of jobs, putting her affairs into some order. Begum Haseeb generally took his advice in all matters. But now there was no one there to consult.

Her son, who was living in London, seemed to be unconcerned. That his sister had married a man of unknown antecedents was her own personal affair. If she had taken a wrong step she must suffer for it. If she had made a correct choice it should make her happy. Everybody is responsible for his own actions; they can bring a man joy or blight his happiness. Begum Haseeb had written her son a long letter to which she had received a two-sentence reply, so casual, so perfunctory, as if nothing had happened.

Alien Heart

Her Pakistani relatives urged her to keep an eye on her younger daughter and send her over to Pakistan. Otherwise she might also fall into a Hindu's clutches. Uncle Zubeir's letter from Pakistan had incensed Zeba. Zahid Bhaijan was any time better than the uncle. He had suggested to Begum Haseeb that after she had passed her High School Examination Zeba should be sent to London for higher studies. Of all persons, Ismet had given Begum Haseeb the greatest surprise. Before Pakistan had come into being Ismet had been prodding her to be ready to migrate to Pakistan. But now though a storm had raged over the Begum's head, Ismet had remained discreetly silent over the whole affair. She just wrote to the Begum once in a while as if her Indian sister-in-law was of no consequence to her. May be this was because her husband was an officer in the Pakistan army and she had to be careful.

Begum Haseeb didn't know what to do.

8

She had guessed right. When the war broke out in Kashmir Ismet had retired into her shell. Normal communications between the two countries had snapped. Ismet's husband was a colonel in the army and the army people had to act under severe constraints.

However, Ismet had managed to send a letter to her sister-in-law with a friend who was visiting India. She had made no attempt to hide her disapproval of what Seema had done; the girl had tarnished the family's fair name. It was all the more reprehensible for she had betrayed them at a time when the Muslims of the subcontinent had made huge sacrifices to bring Pakistan into being. Marrying a Sikh was tantamount to a slap in the face of the entire Muslim brotherhood of Pakistan. It was the Qaid-e-Azam's express desire that no Sikh should be seen in Pakistan.

Ismet had written to her sister-in-law that her husband, colonel Irfan, had sent one of his friends to Amritsar by car and he had managed to meet Seema. He had tried to persuade her to accompany him to Lahore. Ismet had also written to Seema that she should make a trip to Lahore and meet her uncle, aunt and other relatives. But Seema had firmly resisted the proposal and had firmly maintained that she would visit Lahore with Inder alone.

Ismet's husband had made enquiries. His information was that Inder Mohan's father was a bigoted Akali and that his property in Pakistan had been reduced to ashes. Inder's parents had been killed and there was no trace of the remaining members of his family. People said that he had a sister who was in love with a Muslim neighbour and she had stayed back in Pakistan. Nobody knew her whereabouts. Inder Mohan escaped because he was living in Delhi at the time of the holocaust.

Ismet was angry that Seema had refused to visit Lahore at her behest. "Only if once she had stepped into my house, I would not have allowed her to go back," Ismet had written in her letter to the Begum. "I would have forced her into *nikah* with some Muslim youth here. However, I have not lost hope. We shall not rest till we have got the girl out of that hole. Irfan has taken a solemn pledge that he would not allow Seema to live with a Sikh at any cost."

A few days later there was another letter from Ismet. She sounded very happy. She had written that it was now only a matter of days before Seema would be joining her. There had been an agreement between India and Pakistan whereby all the abducted girls in both the countries were to be restored to their respective families. Now those Muslim girls who had forcibly been married to non-Muslims were being located and sent back to Pakistan. Colonel Irfan had managed to get Seema's name included in the list. The department concerned which was entrusted with the job of rescuing such women had promised to raid Seema's house at Amritsar and take charge of her. The Recovery Squad was permitted to go to any village, any town, any city of East Punjab and raid any suspected house with the help of the local police and recover the abducted girls. "I assure you Seema would be with us in Lahore any day," Ismet had written with an air of finality. "You just wait for my next letter. I'm sure it will carry some good news for you."

But many days passed and still there was no letter from Ismet. Begum Haseeb was utterly bewildered. Was Ismet really doing the right thing? Sometimes her spirits revived in the hope that her daughter would be restored to her aunt Ismet. And then her spirits dropped when she realised that her daughter would become a Pakistani citizen and would be lost to her for good. Till now she had not been able to develop any sense of affinity to Pakistan. Her husband had always spoken against it. Now how could she owe allegiance to Pakistan? And then suddenly it made her indignant when she realised that her daughter had married a non-Muslim. The Begum's mind would start wavering. She remained torn between two worlds. She could do nothing but resign herself to circumstances, like a rudderless boat adrift on the sea.

More days passed and still there was no letter from Ismet. She did not know if there had been any further development regarding Seema. Begum Haseeb had cause to worry for Seema was no ordinary girl – she was a determined type. In this she was like her Abba. Once she took a decision, she would not go back on it. She feared that Seema might take some extreme step. She knew Seema was capable of it.

Zeba was even more worried than her mother. Every day she anxiously waited for aunt Ismet's letter. On returning from school her first question was: "Any letter from Lahore?"

The delay only added to Begum Haseeb's anxiety. Zeba too was getting restless. The war in Kashmir still continued.

"What right does India have over Kashmir?" Zeba asked one day in some exasperation. She was going through the day's newspaper.

"What do you mean?" Begum Haseeb reacted angrily.

Zeba stared at her mother in surprise. "Do you have any doubt about it?" she asked. "It's highhandedness on the part of India. To merge Kashmir with India is a big fraud. When it was decided that those regions which had a Muslim majority would go to Pakistan, then to prevent Kashmir from opting for Pakistan is nothing short of a fraud on that country."

"But the Maharaja of Kashmir has proclaimed Kashmir's accession to India," the Begum reminded Zeba.

"Will they give a similar right to the Nizam of Hyderabad? Is Hindu India willing to abide by the verdict on Junagadh?" As usual Zeba's tone was bitter.

"It is Sheikh Abdullah who is responsible for the decision on Kashmir. His party has made this decision."

"Sheikh Abdullah is nothing but a stooge of Pandit Nehru. He is always dancing to his tune," Zeba would not stop arguing.

"Who has been putting such ideas into your head? You are Sheikh Haseeb's daughter and yet you talk as if you were born in a Muslim Leaguer's family."

"Ammi, don't forget that I'm a Muslim." Zeba's voice was full of arrogance. "We young Muslim boys and girls are prepared to die for our rights."

Alien Heart

Begum Haseeb gave her daughter a quizzical look and then looked away. Today this girl was talking with a different voice. She felt as if Zeba had drifted far apart from her. The Begum was already suffering the alienation from her elder daughter and now even her younger daughter was getting estranged from her. They could not see eye to eye with each other on anything. Seema had betrayed her faith and Zeba was now playing false to her own country. She had turned away from her father's ideals. From that evening a wide gulf seemed to separate the mother from the daughter. They tried to avoid each other and the gulf thus kept widening. They lived under the same roof, ate at the same table, and yet they did not seem to have anything common between them.

There was still no news from Ismet. One day Zeba again flared up. "It's all a lie," she said loudly. "Seema Apa should have invented some other lie which could at least sound credible. To say that she married a Sikh because he got hurt while defending her against goondas — this hardly makes sense."

"Zeba, Zeba, please stop tormenting me!" Begum Haseeb pleaded, folding her hands before her daughter.

She picked up her *chaddar* and proceeded towards the family graveyard.

"That day I had come to lament my elder daughter but today I've come to plead on behalf of the younger one." The Begum fell down on the grave of her husband.

9

A surprising change was coming over Zeba. She had started saying namaz and this had greatly pleased her mother. She also went to hold classes for the illiterate Muslim women of the *mohalla*. Every day when her school finished she would go to teach these women, which had again pleased her mother. Many of her classfellows at school often came to her house and held meetings there. They discussed ways of improving the lot of the Muslim residents of the city. Begum Haseeb heartily approved of this.

"I greatly appreciate what you are doing for their betterment," one day Begum Haseeb told Zeba's friend, Mahmood. "But why don't you ask the Hindu boys and girls also to join you?"

"Hindus will tell them to learn Hindi while we teach Urdu to these illiterate folk. There is no arrangement for learning Urdu," Mahmood replied. He was a handsome youth, belonging to a well-to-do family. What he had said had undoubtedly some weight. Ever since Hindi had been declared the official language of the state, Urdu had been pushed into the background. Begum Haseeb had heard that in schools even Muslim children were required to learn Hindi. When an Urdu teacher retired his post was not filled. New schools were being opened just for the purpose of teaching Hindi. No Urdu books were being published and many Urdu magazines and newspapers had closed down. Even the Urdu newspapers that were in existence were influenced by Hindi papers such as *Milap, Pratap, Hind Samachar* and *Tej*, to name only a few.

"Also, Ammijan, we are trying to get jobs for Muslims," Mahmood explained to the Begum. What winsome manners he had and how soft-spoken. "How can Hindu boys help there? We believe that Muslims should get jobs in the police, defence services, in the factories

Alien Heart

and in the other government departments strictly in proportion to their population. For one thing, the places left vacant by the Muslims migrating to Pakistan should have been filled by Muslims alone."

Begum Haseeb was convinced that there was some truth in what Mahmood was saying.

"And, Ammijan, what is of even greater importance is that Muslims should be given full opportunities in business and industry. The government should advance them loans on easy terms and freely issue licences to them to establish new factories and mills. If timely steps are not taken to correct the situation, the Indian Muslims will end up as slaves of the Hindus. We would be living at their mercy. We would have to look to them even for two square meals every day."

Begum Haseeb was inclined to agree with what Mahmood was saying. "Indian Muslims have to live and die in India," she said. "Their destiny is aligned with this country, their interests must be safeguarded. Now they must stop looking to Pakistan."

"But why not? We created Pakistan. Pakistan is our destiny," Mahmood argued.

"You mean you have no responsibility towards your own country?" Begum Haseeb asked in some surprise.

"My country?" Mahmood gave a bitter laugh. "Ammijan, India has been partitioned on the basis of the two-nation theory – the Hindus and the Muslims. Now we have to see whether Hindus will allow remaining Muslims to live here with dignity or not."

Begum Haseeb kept looking at the young man but her mind was somewhere else.

"Indian Muslims have not thrown off the British yoke only to replace it with Hindu shackles. If necessary we shall fight it out. No sacrifice can be too great for this. We are prepared for it. Today all Indian Muslims are united in a common bond." Mahmood's voice rose.

"Son, you think that Zeba's Abba had been deluding himself all his life?"

"Yes, of course. He was a victim of Hindu tricks. This country has not produced a more bigoted Hindu than Mahatma Gandhi. Could there be a more hard-boiled politician than the Mahatma? If Sardar Patel and Pandit Nehru had not put their foot down he would not have allowed Pakistan to come into existence. He was the one who created all the trouble for the Indian Muslims. He always has a Muslim stooge at his beck and call – an Azad, a Kidwai or a Zakir Husain. His intention is to keep the Indian Muslims on the leash. He is out to snatch away their language and fiddle with their jobs. As for trade and industry Muslims have already been sidelined. In course of time they would despite themselves be carried away by the Hindu stream. This is one way of breaking the backbone of a nation."

"I am not sure I understand what you want to say," Begum Haseeb looked at him confused.

"Ammijan, they are teaching Hindi to your daughter at school. Today Zeba is more proficient in Hindi than in Urdu. She folds her hands and says namaste to everyone. I don't see her bowing her head and saying adaab. There was a time when they used to broadcast *naats* and *hamzas*, *qawwalis* and *ghazals* from the Lucknow radio station. Today you hardly hear an Urdu programme over the radio. The language of the news broadcast from All India Radio is becoming more and more unfamiliar as the days pass. The other day someone was saying that these radio people do not broadcast news in Hindi but they propagate Hindi in the news. So far as I am concerned I fail to make much sense of our news bulletins. Every morning and evening I make it a point to tune in to Pakistan Radio for the day's news."

As Mahmood took out a handkerchief from his pocket to wipe his face a wad of hundred-rupee notes came out

Alien Heart

and fell on the floor. He quickly picked up the packet and put it back into his pocket. Then he got up to go. A car had come to fetch him. It was a big, shiny limousine, with a young boy at the wheel. There were other boys and girls in the car.

Since that day Begum Haseeb had relented towards Zeba. The girl was all the time collecting books on Islam and Pakistan. The Urdu programmes from Lahore radio station were most attractive. She tuned in to these programmes morning and evening and listened in to them along with her Ammi.

These days Begum Haseeb drew great comfort by listening to the Quran Shareef broadcast from the Lahore radio station. So many troubles had assailed her all at one time. Recitation of Allah's name gave her great solace. Once she sat down to listen to those qawwalis and hymns, she found it difficult to tear herself away from the radio. In contrast, All India Radio was such a bore – mostly singing of classical music, news read in unintelligible Hindi or broadcasts relating to national development projects. All this just passed over her head.

At long last there was a letter from Lahore from Ismet which had come by hand. Zeba spluttered with rage as she read the letter. The Amritsar police had not permitted the Recovery Squad coming from Lahore to arrest Seema. The contingent had taken away truckloads of abducted Muslim girls from Amritsar proper and from neighbouring villages. But the local police had not allowed them to visit Seema's house, their plea being that nobody could have abducted a graduate girl against her wishes. Besides, Seema's mother was still living in India. The girl's brother might be living in London but he was still a citizen of India. They had property worth lakhs of rupees in Meerut. After the formation of Pakistan no member of their family had migrated to Pakistan. No doubt they had some relations there but they had been living there long before Pakistan came into existence. Ismet had written in her letter: "My husband is not one to admit defeat so easily. He has planned with a member of the Pakistani police to bring back Seema forcibly with the next batch of abducted girls. Once she crosses the border we shall manage the rest." Ismet was confident that her husband would succeed in his mission.

But it seemed that success had again eluded her. As days passed Ismet's hope receded. It appeared they had built an iron wall around Seema which none could demolish. No one could lay hands upon her. She had even stopped writing to her mother. In fact Begum Haseeb herself wanted to break off all connections with Seema. She had developed a prejudice against her. For the last few days she had been struggling with the doubt that maybe her late husband had been following the wrong trail and there was truth in what her younger daughter was dinning into her ears day in and day out. Her doubts were enhanced by the other young men and girls who regularly visited her house and tried to brainwash her.

Then the doctor who was treating Sheikh Shabbir suggested that he should be sent to Pakistan. Maybe that would put the Sheikh in a proper frame of mind and lead to his cure. Even Begum Haseeb sometimes toyed with the idea of migrating to Pakistan. Let the property go to hell. The more important thing was to keep body and soul together for which she had enough money. She felt that if she stayed on in India she might also lose her balance like her brother-in-law. The pendulum of her life was already swinging violently between India and Pakistan.

Begum Haseeb felt utterly confused.

10

At last the Begum made up her mind to migrate to Pakistan. This time she was firm about it. She started looking around for customers for her property. A couple of deals had gone through.

Zeba was pleased, very pleased. And Ismet was the happiest of them all; in her letters she was almost bubbling with joy. Sheikh Shabbir was equally happy. His sister-in-law would enhance his prestige in the community. Her going away would add another feather in his cap. Also, if she stayed back while he went, whenever communal trouble broke out in India or a Pakistani leader made a statement against India, Shabbir would worry about the Begum. She could become the target of communal anger.

Sheikh Shabbir had sold his valuable property for a song. He made satisfactory arrangements to send his cash and gold and jewellery to Pakistan. The only question that remained to be finally decided was as to the place where he would ultimately settle down. All the cities of Pakistan were already overcrowded, with not an inch of space left for the newcomers. A large number of migrants from India were still living in refugee camps. Nobody seemed to be anxious about rehabilitating them. The luckier ones could find shelter with their relatives for ten days, twenty days, a month or even two months. But what would they do after that? They could not be hangers-on for ever.

Sheikh Shabbir's mind was already made up. His people had decided that even if he and his family had to starve they would prefer to die in Pakistan. He would not stay in India a moment longer than necessary because his condition was deteriorating day by day.

When Begum Haseeb's son who was living in London learnt that she was thinking of migrating to Pakistan he strongly advised her against such a step. The conditions in Pakistan, he wrote to her, were none too good. Even those who had migrated there in a hurry were now repenting at leisure. The Panjabis of Pakistan would not allow an outsider to strike roots there. They were specially hostile towards the Muslims of UP whom they contemptuously called "Bhaiyyas". They never tired of making fun of them.

Begum Haseeb was in a dilemma again. As for Zeba, she was all the time praising the fashionable girls of Pakistan. She had several pairs of salwar-kameez stitched for herself. She was particular about the width of the salwar and the girth of the kameez which should conform to the Pakistani style. And, above all, their colour scheme. A shop in the Anarkali bazar of Lahore was named Pazeb and another went by the name of Kahkashan. Zeba had already become knowledgeable with the lay-out of Lahore and bragged to her mother about it.

For many days past Bagum Haseeb had been visiting her husband's grave, where she stayed for hours, talking to him. She would tell him about her woes, hoping that Providence would provide her with a solution. She kept hoping for a bright ray to break through her otherwise dark world. Since the illness of Sheikh Shabbir, she had started feeling quite helpless. There was nobody to advise her. There was nobody in whom she could confide or from whom she could seek guidance. Zeba was no doubt growing into a mature girl but she was a girl all the same. Her mother could not rely upon her entirely. Her advice would sound all right at first but later she would start discovering flaws in it.

And one day there was a bolt from the blue.

That afternoon, waking up from her siesta, the Begum went towards the drawing-room. As she parted the curtain,

Alien Heart

she saw Mahmood sitting on the sofa, and Zeba lying with her head resting on his lap. The Begum immediately retraced her steps and, coming back to her room, fell on her bed.

After some time, when Zeba came into the room, she found her mother in a faint. She had lockjaw and had bitten her tongue from which blood was oozing. There was a large red stain on the bedsheet. The Begum's hands and feet had turned cold and her fingers had got twisted. Zeba forced open her jaws and poured water into her mouth. Then she massaged her hands and feet. Only then did her mother begin to revive.

Though she revived, tears kept pouring from her eyes. She kept staring at Zeba as if the girl had betrayed her in some way. But Zeba proved to be tough. She said that her mother had misunderstood her and that Mahmood was only putting some lotion into her eyes. Her explanations, however, did not convince her mother. She could not disbelieve her own eyes.

At last, in utter desperation, Begum Haseeb decided that she would go away to Pakistan and bear the consequences if things went against her. She would marry off Zeba and absolve herself of the responsibility of looking after a grown-up girl. As for herself, after her husband's death, it was her son's responsibility to take care of her. If need be, she could also live in London with her son.

Begum Haseeb went to Delhi to obtain a permit to visit Pakistan. She thought it would take only a day but she had to prolong her stay to complete the formalities. Everyday she would telephone Zeba to tell her what was holding her up in Delhi. After several days more delay she managed to get permits for herself and her daughter. When the Begum returned home she found Zeba sitting in her room, looking very glum. She told her mother that she had changed her mind and that she would not be going to Pakistan. India was the right place for Indian Muslims to live in. Pakistan already had many problems to cope with. She did not want to add one more. Besides, all the Muslims of India could not possibly migrate to Pakistan. If all the better-off Muslims went away, who would stand by the poorer Muslims who had no choice but to stay behind?

"We have no obligation to others," Begum Haseeb said impatiently. But Zeba was adamant. She refused to budge from her position. The poor widow! She had to obey the dictates of her own daughter! She started unpacking her trunks. Sheikh Shabbir and his family were free to go, if they so desired. She would not stand in their way. But as for herself, it appeared that she was fated to continue to live in Meerut and breathe her last here. She would rest in her grave in this very place.

Not many days had passed when there was a great commotion in the city. The police had raided a Muslim hideout in the local college and unearthed illegal firearms. It had also been able to lay its hand on some printed literature which was to be secretly distributed to the minority community and incite it to violence. Many of the boys had absconded but Mahmood was among those who had been arrested by the police.

Zeba had been secretly advised to slip away to Pakistan before it was too late. When the police got down to its job and applied third degree methods on Mahmood and his accomplices they might let out secrets. Zeba's name was bound to figure prominently for she was an active member of the group. She was probably a party to every recent conspiracy.

Zeba now changed her mind again and said that they should go away to Pakistan. She insisted that they should leave India before the date of their permits expired. "This country cannot be hospitable to Muslims," she claimed. "Specially when Pakistan has come into being on the basis of the Muslims being a separate nation in their own right

Alien Heart

and that they should have a country of their own. On the face of it, it makes no sense for Muslims to persist in living in this country which has become alien to them."

"But it was the Muslim Leaguers who put forward this argument, not the Indians," the Begum countered. "No Congressman wants us to leave India, much less Mahatma Gandhi and Jawaharlal. They always oppose the theory that the Hindus and Muslims are two different nations."

The Begum distinctly remembered what her husband used to say in this regard. "Both Hindus and Muslims would live like good neighbours in India," he used to maintain. "Both are equal citizens of the country. India is a secular State."

"That is nothing but idle talk." Zeba easily scored over her mother in arguments. "As you can see for yourself, Muslims are being butchered all over India. The RSS and Jan Sangh are thirsty for our blood. It's only a question of time when all trace of Muslims will be wiped out from this country. They would be converted to Hindus or become like Hindus. They will speak Hindi and say namaste with joined hands. Muslim girls will use the bindi on their foreheads and produce children for the Hindus and the Sikhs. Like my own sister who is already doing so at Amritsar."

Bagum Haseeb again began making preparations to leave for Pakistan. Just about that time a senior police officer, who was known to the family, called on the Begum and advised her to send Zeba away to another place for some time. Where could she hide a grown-up girl? She decided to leave for Pakistan without further delay.

They had to catch the night train and in the evening the news was flashed that someone had fired three bullets at Mahatma Gandhi and killed him. It had been done because the Mahatma was in sympathy with the Muslims and always stood by them. He had even forced the government to part with fifty-five crore rupees in favour of Pakistan. He had arranged to have coal sent to Pakistan from India because for lack of coal, that country's railways had almost come to standstill. A fanatic Hindu had shot him down.

Begum Haseeb changed her mind once again and stayed put in India.

11

Mahatma Gandhi's death seemed to have cast a spell on Zeba. It changed her thinking altogether. She would no longer let anybody talk disparagingly of him. She acquired a portrait of the Mahatma and hung it in her room. One could see flowers on the portrait all the time – garlands of jasmine and rosebuds. She would often be seen standing with folded hands before the portrait.

Both mother and daughter joined in the last journey of the Mahatma. They formed part of the large concourse, consisting of lakhs who followed the bier, shedding tears.

From that day Zeba began referring to the Mahatma as Bapu. It was like a daughter addressing a father, marked by a note of reverence tinged with tenderness. She had not shown such tenderness even towards her Abba. While addressing Gandhiji as Bapu, Shiekh Haseeb's daughter felt that the whole country was her home. When the Mahatma's ashes were being immersed she went to Allahabad with some of her friends and for many days kept telling her mother about how Babu's ashes were cast into the holy rivers at their confluence.

As before she still went to teach the purdah women in the old town. But she now spoke in a different idiom; it was the language that her father used to speak. She would tell the illiterate women that even before the advent of Muslims there were many religions in India.

Misunderstanding and strife among these religions were not uncommon. But basically all religions were one. All of them preached truth and equality and asked people to lead a clean life. It was the firm belief of the Muslim invaders who had stayed back to rule over India that no religion can be uprooted from the soil of the country. Nor can a ruler rule over a people without their consent. For this reason most Muslim thinkers showed a healthy respect towards the religion of Hindus.

The real trouble started with the coming of the feringis. They sowed the seeds of discord and saw to it that the gulf between Muslims and Hindus kept widening. They kept fanning the flames by inciting one community against the other.

Zeba would also tell them about the fate of Muslims who had migrated to Pakistan, renouncing their own country. Her own uncle had gone to Pakistan after selling all his property in India. He had been among the well-to-do in India and used to have a say in the affairs of the community, but in Pakistan he knocked about from place to place and no one cared for him. He had not been allotted a house to live in, nor a piece of land for cultivation. He could not even find a foothold in business so that he could be on his own.

Qaid-e-Azam Mohammed Ali Jinnah was dead. Liaqat Ali Khan had been assassinated in a public meeting at Rawalpindi. The government had gone all out to probe into the assassination. Nobody could understand why such an eminent figure who was loved by all had been sprayed with bullets. Whenever the Pakistani rulers were confronted with an internal crisis, they diverted the people's attention by raising the problem of Kashmir. They made all sorts of baseless allegations against India. They would say that India no longer stood by the two-nation theory and could invade Pakistan any time and gobble it up. They took care to spread poison against India and keep the illwill simmering.

Begum Haseeb was the most surprised of all when she listened to Zeba. She could not trust her eyes nor believe her ears. Zeba had gone one better than her Abba. Also, she and Seema had started exchanging letters. She had even gone to Amritsar and met her sister there.

A baby was born to Seema. It was a daughter. At the time of her birth Zeba was at Amritsar with her sister. The child closely resembled her maternal grandmother though Seema had taken after her Abba. This was a surprise to Begum Haseeb. She wondered in which niche of her heart Seema had kept the Begum's mother hidden so as to reproduce an exact replica in the person of her own daughter. But Begum Haseeb remained unmoved. She had not yet been able to forgive Seema.

12

The next time when Zeba visited Amritsar she brought Kalu back with her. Like before it took him no time to settle down and make himself at home again. One day Mahmood came to meet Begum Haseeb. Kalu came to tell her about the visitor.

"Begum, a boy has come to meet you."

Alien Heart

"Who's he?"

"I didn't ask his name. But he's handsome fellow."

Begum Haseeb was dressed in just a blouse and petticoat. Now she put on her sari paused before the dressing table for a while to arrange her hair and then went to the drawing-room. She turned pale when she saw Mahmood. Mahmood got up to pay his respects.

"Well?" Begum Haseeb said after a while, breaking the awkward silence.

"When were you released?" She asked. After the police raid, the prosecution proceedings went on for many months and ended with his being sentenced to jail. He had been released a few days back but the Begum was not aware of it.

"I can understand everything, son, except that..." her tongue faltered as she uttered the word 'son' and then trailed off into silence.

"Yes, Ammijan..." How lovingly he was addressing her. It touched a maternal chord in her heart. Then she suddenly recalled that afternoon when she had seen him sitting on the sofa, exactly in the same spot where he was sitting now, with Zeba's head resting in his lap. The girl had looked so radiantly happy. A bitterness spread over every part of Begum Haseeb's body.

"I can understand everything else," Begum Haseeb said. "But I can't tolerate any political movement based on violence." She was speaking in the language of her late husband and echoing the Mahatma's sentiments on which she had been nurtured.

"Ammi, I'm sorry, I haven't followed you." Oh, how softspoken he was, as if he was plucking the strings of a musical instrument. In spite of herself Begum Haseeb turned her gaze on him. She noted his wheatish complexion, the rosy glow on his cheeks, the sparkle in his eyes and a thoughtful far-off look. The Begum's mind was in turmoil. Why didn't she hate this boy who had tried to lead her daughter astray?

"I know that the gap of a whole generation lies between us. But, Ammi, we have not done anything wrong of which we should feel ashamed." His tone was very respectful.

Bégum Haseeb did not say anything. How could she argue with such a softspoken lad? But she had herself seen Zeba's head resting in his lap and her single plait curled upon her breasts. And yet Zeba had insisted that her mother had misunderstood her. That he was just putting some lotion into her eyes! Had Zeba told a lie? Till today she had not retracted her words or admitted her misdemeanour.

Misdemeanour?

The word suddenly became a question mark and stood smiling before the Begum's eyes. She recalled the days of her own youth when she was in love with Sheikh Haseeb. Toba toba! Living in purdah what lies she had had to tell to go out and meet him. But for her Anna's connivance and help she would have never been able to gain her end. She was madly in love with the Sheikh. She was particularly fascinated by the lock of hair that tumbled over his forehead while he was talking.

"But you have not told me what is my fault." Finding the Begum silent, Mahmood repeated his question.

She raised her head and looked at his face. Like Haseeb's a lock of hair had tumbled over his forehead. The Begum got a jolt and her face tingled. "I mean..." she wanted to say something harsh but changed her mind.

"Ammijan, if you are not in a mood to speak out your mind just now, please keep it for some other time. I don't want to disturb you in any way." Mahmood was full of concern for her.

"No, no, son," Begum was immediately disarmed and responded with much tenderness. "I mean I did not

Alien Heart

approve of your party keeping firearms illegally in its office. The police discovered them in the office didn't they?

"Firearms, Ammijan? All your life you have fought against the feringis and still you do not know the tricks of the police?" Mahmood gave her a pained look.

Begum Haseeb stared at him with an abstracted gaze. Such a person was incapable of telling a lie.

"As you know the police had raided our office. They pushed all of us into a separate room and then searched the whole place. After a while, when they opened our room, we saw several revolvers and hand grenades piled in one corner. We had never seen these before."

"What do you mean?"

"It's very clear. The police had planted all those weapons. We were stunned and kept looking at each other."

"You mean those posters and handbills were also not yours?"

"I don't say we had not printed those handbills and posters. We did. But the ones produced by the police in the court were certainly not ours. We had never seen them before."

"You mean our own police can go to such lengths?"

"The police could not have told any bigger lies. Those posters were shocking. The worst of it was that even the language was unidiomatic."

"Even so you were proved guilty and sent to jail."

"Being in jail was not half as bad as the harassment during the interrogation. Ammijan, a moment ago you had said something about violence. What about the police who inflicted all sorts of torture on us?"

"Son, there's no need to tell me about that. We had suffered such torture during the feringi rule."

"But our police has now gone one better than the feringis in this regard."

Mahmood rolled up his sleeve and showed the Begum his arm. It was full of scars as if flesh had been plucked from the arm with pliers.

"You'll find such marks all over my body," Mahmood said. "I was the one who was tortured most. They wanted me to confess that Zeba was our accomplice."

"Son, you should have confessed it. That Zeba was with you is a known fact."

"Yes, Ammijan, every time I was on the point of confessing I changed my mind, I did not want Zeba to be tortured."

"I wouldn't worry about that. But I would be very ashamed if my daughter had been charged with sedition."

"What do you mean, Ammi?"

"I mean that for an Indian Muslim to look to Pakistan in preference to the land of his birth amounts to disloyalty towards his own country."

The Begum saw that Mahmood's face had lost colour.

13

"Mahmood came visiting us," the Begum said when Zeba returned home in the evening.

Zeba ignored her mother's remark.

"Ammi, there's one Mewati among the women whom I go to teach," Zeba told her mother. "Mewatis claim that they belong to the Aryan stock. Although they are Muslims, their customs and way of living are those of the Aryans.

Alien Heart

According to this woman the Mewatis are divided among 12 castes and 52 sub-castes. Her parents belong to Ballabhgarh near Delhi. Their marriages are performed according to the Hindu rites, nikah being a part of those rites. The groom's marriage party stays at the bride's place for three days. The marriages are generally performed in the rainy season and it is forbidden to marry in the same sub-caste. These people worship gods and goddesses and they celebrate *Holi* and observe *Muharram*.

That evening Begum Haseeb was rummaging through her table drawer when she chanced upon a photograph among her old papers. For a moment she mistook it for Mahmood's. The she started smiling. It was her husband's photograph. In his younger days he had looked remarkably like Mahmood. Slim, tall, wheatish complexion, a grave and thoughtful expression on his face, his gaze was fixed on something in the distance. A lock of his hair tumbled over his forehead like Mahmood's did. Their faces looked alike and they talked in the same manner. She had never known her husband to lose his temper nor did he ever raise his voice.

Lost in such thoughts the Begum retired for the night. It was summer and they used to sleep in the courtyard on a raised brick platform under the mosquito nets. Zeba's bed was at some distance from her mother's. The Begum was in the habit of taking a bath, combing her hair and rubbing cold cream on her hands and face before going to sleep. She would slide into sleep as soon as her head touched the pillow.

That night as she lay half-awake she heard Zeba singing in Punjabi:

Man pardesi je thiye
Sub des paraya *

*If the mind is alienated,
The entire country is estranged.

The Begum was deeply moved as if the line had gone straight to her heart.

"Whose saying is this, child?" she asked Zeba.

"It is Baba Nanak's." Zeba sang the couplet again. "Ammijan, I would like the Mussalmans of India to know this utterance, learn it by heart and keep it in their mind." She fell asleep soon after.

It was the rainy season. Rain-heavy clouds were sailing in the sky and the moon sometimes peeped through them as if it was playing hide and seek. As the night advanced a cold wind rose. It must be raining somewhere. Many a time it happened that when there was a downpour at Aligarh, it drizzled in Delhi but Meerut remained dry. The rain-laden clouds would just sail by without shedding their burden.

In her sleep a raindrop fell over Begum Haseeb's cheek. She felt as if she were suddenly drenched. Kalu had returned late after seeing a movie. "Where are you, my moon?" he sang under his breath as he lay on his bed, "Under which clouds are you hiding? Come, my moon!"

"Kudsi!"

"Who, Haseeb?"

"Yes."

"Haseeb, how did you manage to be here?"

"Your Anna showed me the way."

"How dare she?"

"Not so loud. It's past midnight. Everybody is asleep."

He sat down by her side, inside the silky enclosure of the mosquito-net shimmering in the milk-white moonlight. He started playing with her hair like one charmed. He covered her face with its satin softness, coiled the locks round her neck and, proudly pulling her head from under the mosquito-net, showed it to the moon. His face quivered, his fingers tingled, his hands shook. What was he doing? He unbuttoned her blouse and slipped it down

Alien Heart

baring her shoulders. Then the hooks of her brassiere loosened one by one and she lay on the bed with her eyes closed looking like a figure carved in marble. Music played around her in soft, dream-like strains, slowly rising to a crescendo. Who was it singing? There were so many voices, male and female, scores of them, singing together, some in high notes, others in a low key. Then they started dancing, arm in arm, clad in white. It seemed they would float away into the sky while dancing and then descend upon the earth, still dancing. Up and down, down and up. Faster, still faster. Now someone had started throwing *gulal* into the air, one colour emerging from another, red and blue, green and yellow, lustrous and dazzling. She felt as if she were being carried in somebody's arms, she was floating down into some fathomless depth, waves of sleep lapping around her...

Suddenly she heard a scream. Who could it be at this time of the night? It was Zeba. Begum Haseeb came out from under her mosquito-net and leaned over Zeba's bed. Zeba sat there her head resting upon her knees.

"It was him!" Zeba said, speaking with great difficulty.

"Who was it, child?" Pulling the mosquito-net aside the Begum clasped Zeba to her.

"Yes, it was him! The same ..." Zeba stared at her mother.

"But who was he? I don't see anyone around?"

"Mahmood!" Zeba placed her head in her mother's lap. Afrer a while she was fast asleep.

She must have been dreaming. The Begum was sure that it was a dream. But even then she went round the courtyard just to make sure. She looked behind the tree, under the shade of the wall, in the far corner of the verandah. Nobody was there. Kalu was sleeping outside the courtyard, his dog, Dubbu, as usual resting near his charpoy. Not a bird dare move when Dubbu was there.

Yes, it must be a dream. Begum Haseeb returned to her bed. Both mother and daughter had been dreaming!

14

Begum Haseeb had taken a fancy to Mahmood. Why this sudden change? She herself didn't know. She stood alone at the window, searching her heart.

Whose son was he? What were his antecedents? Once or twice the Begum had broached the subject with Zeba. She was not even prepared to hear his name. That day it had led to some unpleasantness. They were having dinner when his name casually came up. "I like the boy," the Begum had said.

"In that case you might as well..." Zeba was nearly impertinent. These days she would fly into a tantrum over nothing. She got up from the table without finishing her dinner. Under such circumstances, it was certainly a bit odd for Begum Haseeb to take interest in the young man. But the fact was that as she stood in the window looking at the wide lawn stretched below her, her thoughts were concentrated on Mahmood.

Kalu was at the back of the house teasing the milkman. "I hope you don't add Hindu water to your milk," he said to the vendor. "These days none can trust a man who wears a tuft on his head. Be good enough not to defile my Begum's dharma. If you must adulterate the milk, do it with water from a Muslim pitcher."

"How you talk! Do you think I'll not be answerable to God for my actions in the next world? Specially these days when there is no love lost between Hindus and Muslims?" The milkman laughed and added, "I take care to mix the milk with tap-water supplied by the municipality. And I mix it in the right proportion."

"Hindus are a clever lot. They sanctify even the municipal tap."

"But my cow is a Muslim. I had bought it from the Sheikh Serai cattle market."

"How can a cow be a Muslim? A cow is born a Hindu and dies a Hindu."

"That's why I say you must always have buffalo's milk."

"You should be thankful that the Mahatma's followers have not persuaded her to drink goat's milk."

They were all there, the cook, the *mali* the sweeper, having a dig at one another.

The Begum realized it had become a habit with her again to stand at the window. She used to plant herself at the window like that waiting for her husband's return. Her whole life had become a long wait. It was like a rosary, the passing moments its beads. They represented long and short periods of waiting. There were periods of unending wait and shorter ones which found quick fulfilment. She would see her husband's car entering the gate and stopping under the porch. Sometimes she heard the hooves of the horses drawing his buggy. She had also seen him being led out by the police after his arrest. There were happier occasions too when he was loaded with garlands and led to the house in a procession, the air full of the cries of 'Inqilab zindabad!'

She was standing at the window lost in thought when she saw the gate opening and Mahmood walking in. He was wearing a white khadi kurta and pyjamas. On his feet he wore *chappals*. As he entered through the gate he tossed back his long hair, in the same manner as her husband used to. Like her husband, he was also walking with downcast eyes, absorbed in thought. Her husband's habit of walking with his head bent low made his hair fall over his forehead and he would toss it back with a jerk of his neck.

"Why don't you have your hair clipped short?" she would ask her husband.

"Where's the time for it?" he would reply.

I think you don't want to trim your hair until our country gains independence," she would tease him.

Then she found herself sitting with Mahmood in the drawing-room, telling him about her husband's quaint ways. Mahmood's face reddened for he realised that his hair had also grown long and required clipping.

"We have yet to gain independence," he said pushing back his hair.

"What do you mean?"

"Ammi, the Indian Muslims are like hostages. Perhaps you don't know that Hindu-Muslim riots have already started in Aligarh."

"Hai, Allah! When did this happen?" Begum Haseeb was horrified. Her parents lived in Aligarh.

"This morning." His tongue faltered a little.

"How did the riots start?" Begum Haseeb was anxious to know.

"Do the communalists need a reason to start a riot? Any excuse will do." Mahmood said in a carefree tone as if a communal riot could be started casually, like children falling out while at play.

"There must have been casualties. You know my parents live in Aligarh?"

"In which locality?"

"Near the university."

"Then they are safe. The riots have started in the city."

"But what was the immediate provocation?"

Alien Heart

"The question of roti. The Hindu wants to snatch away the Mussalman's roti from his mouth. The Hindus of Aligarh insist that from now on they won't allow Muslim craftsmen to make brass idols of Hindu gods and goddesses, which they have been making for generations."

"But that makes no sense."

"Sense or no sense, the quarrel started over it."

"And what's the police doing about it?"

"The police is a silent spectator. It just watches the fun. Or it joins hands with Hindus in burning down our houses and shooting down unarmed Muslims."

"How can that be possible?"

"Ammijan, that is exactly what is happening. The lanes of your beloved parents' town are flowing with blood. The corpses of Muslims are rotting in the gutters. Nobody can come out of his house while the curfew is on."

"Such a thing has never happened before. I have never heard of such a thing happening anywhere."

"The entire police force consists of Hindus. All the Muslim officers and policemen who migrated to Pakistan have been replaced by Hindus. No Muslim has now any chance of entering the army or the police!"

"I can't believe it."

"But Ammi, it's a fact. Your daughter has done her B.A. and she's sitting idle for want of a job. And here, right in front of you, you have a young man who has done his M.A. and has been looking for a job ever since."

"Such a condition is really unbearable?"

"There's not much to choose between Nehru and Azad. They are cast in the same mould. They have forgotten their old promises. Nobody cares for the minorities. There is no place for Muslims in India. They just can't survive here."

Mahmood kept talking in this vein till Begum Haseeb got tired of listening to him. She felt as if she had become defiled, a bad smell had started assailing her nostrils. She sat lost in thought long after Mahmood was gone.

Then Zeba came in. Her mother looked agitated. Zeba wanted to know what was worrying her mind. The Begum told her about the riots in Aligarh. Zeba had heard no such thing. And there was no news about it over the radio either.

"The radio also belongs to the government. It speaks its master's voice." Begum Haseeb still looked very worried. She had purposely not told Zeba that Mahmood had brought her the news.

When there was no such news even in the evening news bulletin, Zeba phoned up Aligarh. The call did not materialize. She waited and waited in vain and then went to sleep.

15

The next morning radio news-bulletin mentioned the riots in Aligarh. The radio said that the riots had started all of a sudden last night. The morning's newspapers also featured the Aligarh riots.

The houses in the narrow lanes of the city were being looted and burnt. People were stabbing each other in the bazars, while sporadic firing was going on. Some said that Muslims were the worst sufferers, while others maintained that Hindus had been massacred in large numbers. Some believed that this time Muslims had started the riots, while others said that Hindus were to blame. A curfew had been clamped over the entire city and the police was rounding

Alien Heart

up the goondas. But most of them had already gone underground. There was tension among the students. The university had been closed and the examinations postponed. The army had been asked to keep in readiness and police contingents from other districts had been sent for to assist the Aligarh administration. Even some central ministers had decided to visit the town. The Prime Minister had severely denounced the riots in a statement made in Delhi. The citizens of Aligarh had been asked to form peace committees.

The newspaper fell down from the Begum's hand even while she was reading it. Communal riots always started like this without any warning. It would take the police by surprise as much as the general public. It always ran to a set pattern. In each locality, the community having the majority came down with a heavy hand on the community which happened to be smaller in number. Curfew was ordered in the area and the police put on the alert. When the situation worsened the army was called in and the state ministers dutifully arrived on the scene. A statement was issued from Delhi and peace committees were formed. The Begum wondered why, although all possible precautions were taken, still the riots broke out. The poor suffered the most and the innocent died. After some time, as the riots petered out, enquiry committees were promptly formed and that was the end of it. Their findings were put in cold storage.

The riots in Aligarh were running to the same pattern as Mahmood had told her. However, when she mentioned this to Zeba that evening, she pulled a long face. Zeba had had an early breakfast and gone out, not even caring to read the newspaper for she had already got the news over the radio. If Aligarh was in the grip of rioting, it could also spark off trouble in Meerut. But Zeba was a fearless girl. She had set out from home so early in the morning and there was no knowing when she would return. Begum

Haseeb thought that if she could meet Mahmood, she could ascertain the facts from him. But how to find him? Maybe Kalu knew where to reach him. There was nobody in the city whom Kalu did not know. She had guessed right. Just one word from her and Kalu rode out on his bicycle and brought Mahmood home with him.

As long as Mahmood was with the Begum he kept denigrating the Hindu community and praising the Qaid-e-Azam. According to him, Indian Muslims were being given stepmotherly treatment. The communal riots would continue until the Muslims were given their rightful share in the government services. They were also to be given proper incentives in business and industry.

Begum Haseeb could readily grasp the implications of what Mahmood was saying. Recruitment of Muslims to the police would put a curb on the cruelty being inflicted on the minorities. And if Muslims ran their own factories and had a share in trade and commerce, they would as much be afflicted by the goondas and the arsonites as Hindus. But what Begum Haseeb found most disturbing was Mahmood's constant harping on Pakistan as if his gaze was all the time fixed on something beyond the Indian border. He could see nothing wrong in the Pakistani political leaders and his sympathies lay with the people there. He had a rational explanation for every lapse on the part of Pakistan and in contrast he magnified every shortcoming of India. It seemed while his body was in India his heart was in Pakistan. In the course of his long talk with the Begum he had not even once claimed India as his own country.

Begum Haseeb felt uncertain. Mahmood's attitude was so unpleasant, yet somehow she could not dislike him. On the other hand his talk whetted her interest. She asked him to stay for lunch. In the course of their talk she learnt that Mahmood's father owned a lot of land outside the city. The government had acquired some portion of it to set up a power house there. He had been compensated for it, the amount running into a few lakhs. Yet he had filed a case against the government. He had lost in the lower court and had now appealed to the High Court. His lawyer had assured him that he would win the case for him and get him another couple of lakhs by way of compensation. He grew vegetables on the rest of the land.

"But why vegetables only"? Begum Haseeb asked. "Why not some other crops?"

"Because one can easily dispose of vegetables and quit the place."

"What do you mean?"

"You never know when we may have to leave India."

The ground seemed to slip from under the Begum's feet as she heard Mahmood's explanation. What strange notions some people had.

"At first we used to grow wheat and, later on, paddy. But now we grow cauliflowers, tomatoes and other seasonal vegetables. Grow them today and sell them off tomorrow. Cash crops!"

"What do your brothers and sisters do?" Begum Haseeb asked.

"I have only one sister," Mahmood replied. "Ammijan has gone away to Pakistan with her. If she can find a suitable match for her there, she will marry her off."

"But couldn't she find a suitable boy for her in India?"

"Ammi, do you think there is any worthwhile Mussalman left in India now?"

"Why, I see one sitting right in front of me." Begum Haseeb gave Mahmood a meaningful look, as if she had already succeeded in conveying her mind to him. Pleased with herself, she got up and went to the kitchen.

Begum Haseeb's remark buoyed up Mahmood's spirits. Sitting alone in the drawing-room, he thought his misunderstanding with Zeba would soon come to an end. Her mother was now on his side; he had already won her goodwill. Her 'vote' was in his pocket. Now Zeba could not slip out of his grasp even though she was a headstrong girl. For that matter, every good-looking girl is headstrong, self-willed, and arrogant. If he could get a girl like Zeba for a wife, he would ask for nothing more. She would prove such a big prop to his party. He feared that if she went about like this for some time more, she might fall into the hands of a Hindu. One sister of hers had already disgraced herself and her family; the other could also go astray. But the fact of the matter was that the fault did not lie with these girls. In the first place their father had been so liberal and in the second place a widow's children were always prone to become wayward.

Mahmood was really surprised when he was called to eat. Begum Haseeb had laid such a nice table, loaded with delectable food, kabab and korma, biryani and chutney of curds. They had just started eating when Zeba came in. Her eyebrows went up on seeing Mahmood sitting at the dining-table. "I'm sorry for being late. A friend of mine detained me for lunch." After talking with them for a few minutes, she went away to her room.

Mahmood had just left after finishing his meal when Begum Haseeb saw Zeba sitting at the dining table, eating her food.

She has taken after her father, Begum Haseeb said to herself.

16

While eating her food it occurred to Zeba that it must be Mahmood who had told her mother about the Aligarh riots. According to the news given by the radio and the newspapers, the riots started only last night. How could Mahmood get the news before the actual trouble started? She wanted to ask her mother who had first given her the news about the riots at Aligarh. But she had begun detesting Mahmood so much that she did not even wish to utter his name before her mother. Her mother on the other hand had started doting on Mahmood and went to the extent of feasting and pampering him.

Zeba was eating alone. The servants had retired. Zeba had gone to the kitchen and served herself. The mother and daughter were alone in the dining-room.

"Beti, you should have eaten with us," the Begum said, "The food must be cold."

"Ammi, you know very well that I don't like this man," Zeba said trying to sound matter-of-fact.

"But what's wrong with him? I should also like to know." The Begum was really anxious to know the secret of her daughter's dislike for the young man. There was a time when Zeba doted on Mahmood. She had herself seen the two of them together in the drawing-room in a situation that did not suggest Zeba disliked Mahmood.

Zeba ignored her mother's question. She poured water into her glass from the jug and drank it.

"He comes of an affluent family. He is educated, tall and handsome."

Zeba remained silent.

"These days it is so difficult to come across good boys. His mother has herself gone to Pakistan in search of a young man for his sister."

Zeba kept eating in silence. She only glanced at her mother.

"How softspoken he is. And well behaved. How sweetly he calls me Ammi."

Zeba pitied her mother. It was the same mother who had fainted on seeing her head resting in his lap.

"If you have someone else in mind, you must tell me. I am your mother. I don't believe in interfering in my children's affairs."

"Ammi, why are you in such a hurry? If you want to get rid of me I can leave the house on my own."

"You blurt out whatever comes into your head. Stop talking nonsense."

Zeba laughed.

"I mean there's a time for everything. Your studies are over. You must now prepare for the next stage of your life."

"You mean I must make a home for someone? See his children playing in the courtyard. And then his children's children. My poor country! My India!"

"You will soon find yourself left behind. It's people like you find fault with everything and then miss the bus in life. You must think coolly over the matter. You have our neighbour, the Khan Bahadur's daughter's example before you. Her hair has turned grey and yet she remains unmarried. There was a time when eligible young boys swarmed around her and longed for her hand. Now no one even looks at her."

"So what, Ammi? Kammo Apa now teaches in a school. I think she is quite happy with her lot."

"Don't you see how she rides her bicycle, her legs going up and down on the pedals on the way to school. If she had married she would have been going about in a car. She would have had a home of her own and servants to dance attendance on her. The girls of her age have now become mothers. Their children study in her school. They call her 'Auntie'."

Zeba had finished her meal but her mother had not finished her sermon.

"Ammi, I give you my pledge," Zeba said, wiping her hands on the towel. "I'll not bother you about my marriage."

Tears came to the Begum's eyes.

"Beti, if your Abba were alive, I wouldn't have worried over anything. But now all these responsibilities have fallen upon my shoulders. My son is living so far away. I keep looking out for his letters till my eyes start aching."

Zeba was deeply moved on seeing tears in her mother's eyes. The Begum was shrewd enough to realise that now was the time to draw out her daughter.

"But tell me frankly what's wrong with this boy, Mahmood?"

Zeba said nothing.

"Whenever I mention his name, you withdraw into your shell. At least I must know what the reason is." Begum Haseeb seemed determined to take a decision once for all.

"Ammi, I have seen Mahmood from very close quarters. He's the wrong type of person so far as I'm concerned."

"There's always one thing or another wrong with a man. It's in their very nature. No one is perfect." It was the Begum's own experience speaking.

"True, there are some faults which can be overlooked. But there are some which cannot be ignored. One cannot condone a man for them."

"But I must know what these faults are. Why can't you be specific?"

"Mahmood, his mother, his Abba live in this country like aliens."

"I've also felt the same about Mahmood at times. He is always looking beyond the Indian border. But why should that worry you? There are so many other Muslims like him. Time will teach them what is better."

"Not people like Mahmood. They'll never learn. These people are like birds getting ready for flight. They can go any moment and land across the border."

"But the majority community in our country has a responsibility towards the minorities. It can't trample their rights underfoot."

"I'm sick of hearing this all the time," Zeba said with an edge to her voice. "Why should the minorities have all the rights? The majority community surely has some rights too."

"Take the case of language. As far as Urdu is concerned, I feel that the government's neglect is deliberate."

"In the case of Urdu the neglect is in fact on the part of its champions."

"Is it not because the government is forcing Hindi upon them?"

"That's exactly my complaint. Why shouldn't the majority community foster and promote its language? Why can't we give our neighbours the same right which we demand for ourselves? Their only fault is that they are in a majority."

"I believe that language is one reason why the Muslims in India have set their eyes on Pakistan."

"Is Pakistan not trying to impose its language upon East Pakistan? They say that if you don't want to give up your language, you must at least adopt the Persian script for it. On this score many Bengalis have been shot dead in Dhaka. If the Pakistanis can force the Bengalis to read Urdu, then what's wrong if we are asked to learn Hindi? The Pakistanis are thinking of merging Kashmir with Pakistan. I fear, at this rate, they may lose even their East Bengal."

Zeba was talking in an impassioned tone. Begum Haseeb thought it discreet to drop the subject at that point.

17

The conditions in Aligarh were still far from normal. The curfew was still imposed at night. One morning Zeba suddenly announced that she was going to Aligarh to meet her grandparents. Being the headstrong girl she was there was no stopping her. She would have her way.

Normally it would have been proper for Begum Haseeb to accompany her daughter to Aligarh, but she was not in favour of leaving her house under the present circumstances. Besides, she had taken a fancy to Mahmood and she wanted to tie him to Zeba. The only snag and a big one at that was that Zeba would not tolerate it. However, the Begum was still hopeful; she thought she could bring Zeba round in due course. In such matters the opinion held by girls really does not count and they can ultimately be prevailed upon, so the Begum thought. Mahmood was educated and came from a rich family. What more did Zeba want? As for his being a fanatic, perhaps it was all to the good, for it had saved him from forming some other vicious connection. When in a critical mood, her husband used to say, "Under his skin every Hindu belongs to the Hindu Mahasabha, every Indian Muslim is a Muslim Leaguer and every Sikh is an Akali at heart. Rarely, if ever do we come across a Congressite. The only persons who can genuinely claim to be Congressites are Mahatma Gandhi, Jawaharlal Nehru, Maulana Azad and Rafi Ahmed Kidwai. And there the tally more or less ends."

That evening Mahmood had dropped in to meet Begum Haseeb. Since Zeba's departure for Aligarh, he often came to meet the Begum. Although a mother of grown-up children, the Begum had retained her feminine charm and had taken pains to preserve it. She had a way about her, a bold openness without any taint. She had large laughing eyes and a broad glowing forehead. Some strands that had turned grey seemed to enhance the darkness of her hair. Her figure was tall and stately like that of a Mughal queen. That evening she wore a *gharara* and a *chikan* kurta and had draped a silk *chunri* over her head. A faint fragrance followed her as she entered the room.

She seemed to have cast a spell over Mahmood. The tea over, she herself prepared a *paan* for him. Mahmood wished that she should keep on talking; her words fell on his ears like the swing of music to which he seemed to have become attuned. She said, "True, Jinnah was one of the founders of the Muslim League but he was the most progressive of the Leaguers. Had he lived for some time more, he would not have allowed Pakistan to become a Muslim state. He had always said that after the formation of Pakistan, no citizen would have a separate entity as a Muslim, a Hindu or a Christian. They would all be Pakistanis." In 1934 Jinnah had said, "I'm first an Indian and then a Muslim." On 11th August, 1947 he had said before the Constituent Assembly of Pakistan, 'Whether one goes to worship in a temple, a mosque or a church, or whether one professes a certain religion or belongs to a certain caste or community, it has nothing to do with that individual's fundamental rights. We are all equal citizens of one country.'

"In Pakistan every fifth child becomes the victim of hunger. I had read somewhere that in 1949-50 an average Pakistani citizen ate 2,010 calories which had now been reduced to 1,970. According to a news item in the *Pakistan Times* someone in Jhelum had sold his son for twenty-two rupees so that his parents could procure food for four days to ward off death. In West Pakistan 6,000 farmers had more land than 33 lakh peasant families put together.

"In Pakistan there is no freedom of the press. Newspapers like the *Pakistan Times*, the *Imroz*, the *Lailonihar* have been taken over by the government. General Ayub says that democracy does not suit the climate of tropical countries. Democracy, according to him, can only thrive in countries with a cold climate. When the attention of a minister of Pakistan was drawn towards the vast mass of illiterates in the country, he retorted that even the Prophet was unlettered.

"Pakistan treats East Bengal like a colony even though the Bengalis outnumber the people of West Pakistan. The language of East Bengal is being suppressed. Every year West Pakistan gobbles up crores of rupees earned by East Pakistan by way of foreign exchange. From 1948 to 1951 only 22 per cent of the total development funds were spent on East Pakistan. How long can these people put up with this open exploitation? The boat is sure to rock one day. The Bengalis are not going to put up with the tyranny of West Pakistan for long.

"And now we learn that they are forging a friendship with America. And it's only a friendship in name for Pakistan has sold itself to America for the sake of food and military hardware. They have actually mortgaged their country to America. In 1950 Liaqat Ali Khan went on a visit to America and in 1951 American dollars started flowing into Pakistan like water. He also brought with him American experts and advisers. The American foreign policy became the foreign policy of Pakistan, the latter towing the line in every manner. Today the American dollar completely dominates the policies of Pakistan. Friendship with America means that Pakistan should cultivate friendship with only those countries that are friendly with America—South Vietnam, South Korea, Formosa."

It was like a picture speaking. Mahmood listened to Begum Haseeb spellbound, his face bright with understanding. Every sentence that the Begum had spoken seemed to have left its mark on him. His head was not prepared to accept at value what Begum Haseeb had said and yet he was listening to her with rapt attention, as if his heart was not willing to contradict the Begum. What a sweet mother she was, fostering in him a deep sense of belonging. She must have been ravishingly beautiful in her younger days.

Mahmood wanted to know why, if the Congress was not communal-minded, did it always make it a point to put up a Muslim candidate from a Muslim dominated constituency? It did so for the Panchayat elections as much as for the Assembly and Parliament. Even Maulana Azad was returned from Haryana with Muslim support. But Mahmood did not say all this to her. He just kept gaping at her like some guilty man standing in the dock.

"I agree that we Indians are not angels," Begum Haseeb said, realising that Mahmood was finding himself vulnerable. "We have always held before the people Shivaji as a symbol of Hindu heroism forgetting that he spent all his life fighting against the Mughals. And we also conveniently forget that the keeper of his arsenal was a Muslim. Maharaja Ranjit Singh had deputed a Muslim commander to fight against his Muslim adversary at Multan. The Maharaja's adviser in external affairs was also a Muslim. Many Muslim rulers had a hand in constructing Hindu temples. Mohammed Shah, the ruler of Delhi, assigned an estate to the Bodhi temple at Gaya. One of the biggest estates of India, Darbhanga, had been bequeathed by Emperor Akbar to a Brahman in recognition of his learning. The ruler of Kashmir, Zain-ul-Abedin, regularly went on a pilgrimage to Amarnath. Till the other day a Brahman was the trustee of a Muslim shrine in the Nizam's dominion and the Nizam himself was a frequent visitor to that shrine.

"In Punjab, Bihar and Assam there is hardly any difference in the mode of living of Hindus and Muslims. Both wear the same type of dress and sing the same folk songs and tell the same folk tales. I also agree with the view that the communal riots both in India and Pakistan are deliberately foisted on the Hindus and Muslims to divert their minds from the internal lapses and shortcomings of the governments. In some places prices are rising and at others unemployment is growing, while the gulf between the rich and the poor widens."

The evening had advanced and darkness crept over the house. Begum Haseeb had just stretched out her hand to switch on the light when Mahmood got up. He felt as if someone had popped a sugar-coated quinine tablet into his mouth. He had had enough of it for the day. He could not assimilate any more. But Begum Haseeb would not stop speaking in her engaging manner.

As soon as he stepped out of the Begum's house, he shrugged off the Begum's words just as an ass shakes off drops of water from its back. "She'll soon know better," Mahmood said to himself. "She has not seen the seamy and sordid side of life. Even if she has, it has not touched her in a raw spot. She has lost one daughter for good and the other can also slip out of her hands. It's only then that she will learn."

18

Zeba's maternal grandfather lived on Naqvi Road between the city and the university campus in Aligarh. The curfew had not been relaxed in the city and the tension had not abated. One could still hear gunfire at night. There were still stray cases of stabbing; some poor people caught defenceless while going alone were knifed to death.

The sudden cries of 'Har Har Mahadev!' and 'Allah-Ho-Akbar!' still rent the air. Provocative posters written in Hindi inciting Hindus to action had been plastered on the city walls, while there were also posters printed in Urdu similarly inciting the gullible Muslims. The Muslim mohallas had 'Pakistan Zindabad!' painted across the walls which the police made a point to erase. But no sooner their backs were turned than someone would again write the same message on the same wall. This game of hide and seek went on in the city.

It was getting dark when Zeba reached her maternal grandparents' place. To her surprise, a game of badminton between young boys and girls was in progress in the lawn with old men and women sitting around watching the game. Their neighbour, Rai Saheb Ram Jawaya, was there with members of his family. Sardar Nasib Singh's son and daughter who lived across the road in a bungalow were playing. As the light faded, electric lights were switched on.

"I am amazed. I thought that your city was in the grip of riot," Zeba said as she went round greeting her relatives and neighbours.

"Of course, the riots are on but so is our game," Sardar Nasib Singh's Panjabi wife said, "Both the games must go on."

"Perhaps these people have nothing better to do," Zeba's aunt said. She was an Andhrite, from Hyderabad.

"Bibi, may I have a paan?" Sardar Nasib Singh's wife said. "You are responsible for my paan-eating habit."

"It's tit for tat. You have made us lassi addicts. My husband refuses to eat unless there is a mug of lassi on the table."

The game over, Rai Saheb Ram Jawaya's daughter, Swarna, came out of the court with her brother Rajiv. She hugged Zeba. They were old friends. Zeba also knew Rajiv but they had not met for many years for he had been

Alien Heart

away in England for his education. He had grown into a handsome young man and had returned after doing his F.R.C.S. Raising her right hand, Zeba bowed slightly, trying to greet him in the Awadhi style. But before she could do that Rajiv advanced and took her hand in his own. "You remember, last time we had a verse contest on this very lawn and you had defeated me and two of my other friends? Is your stock of Urdu verse still as large?"

Zeba easily recalled that moonlit summer night. They were vying with one another reeling off verses on the lawn. She was one against three and yet she had been able to score over them. This was many years ago. Oh, how she had recited couplet after couplet!

"I'm game even today," Zeba laughed. Her hand was still in Rajiv's hand, a young girl's hand in the grip of a handsome young man! For a fleeting moment they looked into each other's eyes and Zeba's hand shook like mercury.

"I hear now you are also required to study Hindi as a compulsory subject."

"That's nothing to worry about. I've been standing first in my class in Hindi."

"Good heavens! Then you are of no use to us."

"In my opinion, Devanagri is the most scientific script."

"Not scientific but linguistically perfect," Swarna commented.

"That's where I disagree with you."

Zeba's aunt offered paan to Swarna and Rajiv. Rajiv let go Zeba's hand.

"You don't eat paan?" Rajiv asked Zeba.

"Of course I do. But after you."

Rajiv offered Zeba his own paan which she readily accepted.

"I've been here only seven days," Rajiv said, settling down in a chair. "Oh, how time flies!"

"No, six days, not seven," Swarna corrected her brother.

"Oh, yes, six days. Rioting started the same night as I arrived. On the night between Sunday and Monday. Today is Saturday. That makes six days."

"Did the riots start on the night between Sunday and Monday or between Saturday and Sunday?" Zeba asked, looking a bit startled.

"On the night between Sunday and Monday," Swarna said. "Was there any previous incident which could have provoked the riots?"

"I don't think so."

"Yes, Rajiv had reached home by that time. We had just finished our dinner when there was a phone call from the Superintendent of Police to say that rioting had started in the city."

Zeba became lost in thought. She clearly remembered that it was Sunday evening when she returned home her mother had mentioned the riots at Aligarh. And then she had made a phone call to Aligarh which did not materialise.

Rajiv's observant eyes did not fail to notice Zeba's mood. "Miss Sheikh, why are you looking so grave? You seem to think the riots should have started much earlier than they actually did?" His remark drew a laugh from them all.

"Exactly, that's what is puzzling my mind," Zeba said in a halting tone.

"What do you mean?" Swarna asked.

"I clearly remember that last Sunday when I returned home in the evening, Ammi told me that Hindu-Muslim riots had started in Aligarh. And after that I had made a phone call to Aligarh."

"I'll tell you what," Rajiv laughed. "It could be some sort of intuition at work. For the people who are used to cutting their neighbours' throats year after year coming events cast their shadows before them. I myself at times

Alien Heart

get a premonition of what is coming. My heart starts sinking before the actual event overtakes me. Or I start feeling irritated without any apparent rhyme or reason."

"Just as you were feeling today," Swarna teased her brother.

"When?"

"Didn't you have a tiff with me while having tea?"

"Yes, I had got into a nasty mood for no reason." Rajiv said, suddenly becoming thoughtful.

"It seems something untoward had cast its shadow in advance?" Zeba asked in a light-hearted vein.

"Maybe, but I didn't mark anything unusual this evening."

"Except your meeting with Zeba!" Swarna said. And they all started laughing.

19

In Zeba's absence Mahmood came to visit the Begum almost every day. On the day he did not show up, the Begum would herself send for him. He was generally invited to stay for lunch if he came in the forenoon, and for dinner if he happened to be there in the evening.

Begum Haseeb would at times make him run small errands for her. Now that Mahmood was regularly visiting her, Begum Haseeb would try to keep the house spick and span. She would put fresh flowers in the vase every day. One day Mahmood had told her in passing that he did not like the smell of incense sticks. It reminded him of a Hindu temple. From that day Begum Haseeb stopped burning incense sticks in the house, although she had been filling her house with their fragrance all her life. She had the lawn moved every other day and asked the mali to tend the garden morning and evening. The water carrier had been particularly instructed to sprinkle water right from the gate upto the porch to keep the dust from blowing. There must not be a speck of dust in the air, she had warned him.

Strangely enough, she herself was getting estranged from herself. On waking up she liked to stay in bed and have her morning cup of tea. This was a new trait in her for she was an early riser and prepared her morning tea herself. These days she spent a long time in the bathroom. After many years she had once again become choosy about her clothes, taking a long time to decide what to wear for the day. She would keep redoing her clothes, sometimes loosening a blouse and at others tightening a kurta. Coming out of her bath, she would keep her hair loose for as long as she fancied. Previously she used to put on the radio just for the news but these days she forgot to switch it off after the news bulletin was over. She seemed to have developed a taste for film music. When alone, Begum Haseeb would search her mind. What was happening to her? She stayed awake long into the night and kept gazing at the stars through the window. All sorts of film songs kept echoing in her ears.

Last Thursday she had forgotten to light a candle at her husband's grave. Even the previous Thursday too she had made the same lapse. When she thought of it she shook from head to foot and sweat broke out on her body.

Then she saw the gate opening and Mahmood walking in. She rushed into the dressing room. The next moment it was a smiling Begum greeting her guest.

She read out to him some excerpts from a newspaper report. The government had announced some schemes to

Alien Heart

open up avenues of employment for the people. One such scheme related to skilled workers and technicians. They would be given the benefit of refresher courses in their specific trades. The more promising of them would go in for diploma and degree courses. There had been a spate of applications from those interested in these schemes. Many candidates among them had been given loans, some of them to the tune of two lakhs each, so that they could set up their own small enterprises. But, curiously enough, there were no Muslim applicants among the aspirants. There was only one solitary application for a loan which was duly accepted. "Are we to conclude from this that there is no unemployment among the Muslims?" asked Begum Haseeb.

Mahmood gave a bitter laugh. "Ammijan, you are very simple," he said. "This is official hand-out, mere propaganda."

"But this is not an official hand-out." Begum Haseeb threw the paper in Mahmood's direction.

"Then it must have been cooked up by some interested party or some government stooge," Mahmood said without glancing at the paper.

"It must be the brainwave of some wretched Hindu," Mahmood said in a derisive tone, knitting his eyebrows before Begum Haseeb could open her mouth.

"But the writer is a Muslim." Begum Haseeb picked up the newspaper from Mahmood's knees and held it before his eyes.

Mahmood refused to read the newspaper.

"You just don't know how the Hindus are bent upon wiping us Muslims out of existence," Mahmood said in a bitter tone. "They are right in a way. We have our Pakistan. Our rightful place is in Pakistan."

"But does Pakistan also subscribe to this view? The Pakistanis detest Indian Muslims. They have even restricted their entry into Pakistan." Begum Haseeb taunted him.

"Of course, they are right. The people migrating from India want land for land and business in exchange for business. Who would care to share his property with someone else?"

"Then what are you Indian Muslims gloating over?"

"That's the whole trouble. It's we who brought Pakistan into existence. It's we who made sacrifices for it. But it is the Panjabis who have usurped it."

"Yes the Muslim League could never form a government in Punjab before independence came."

"We shall have to fight one more battle."

"On this side or that?"

"On both sides. Here and across the border." Mahmood got up and proceeded towards the bathroom.

The boy was becoming a bit of an enigma for the Begum. But some of the things he had said she did not find so unpalatable as before. She would readily listen to him. She had become more receptive to his ideas. There was a time when she openly disapproved of what he said and minced no words about it. She would even plug her ears with her fingers and even feel like slapping him for the sacrilege that he so easily mouthed.

Yesterday she had decided that if Mahmood dropped in at an odd hour, she would not ask him to stay back for dinner. What would the servants be thinking? While standing before the mirror in the morning she had said to herself: "This boy is fast becoming your weakness." And then her face had suddenly turned pale. Surely, people must be talking about it. But this time she again detained Mahmood for dinner.

"Mahmood Mian will have dinner," she told the cook raising her voice.

As usual they fell to talking. The Begum recited a couplet from Jalaludin Roomi. Mahmood did not know Persian. The Begum translated the couplet for his benefit:

I have extracted the essence from the Quran.

And have thrown away the bones to the dog.

"What do you mean?" Mahmood gave her a quizzical look.

"It is necessary to understand the quintessence of Islam," the Begum said, "It's no use quarrelling about the inessentials."

20

A dense, dark night. Bitterly cold. A wild storm raging outside as if it was going to uproot everything. A thick fog lay over the streams, ponds and tanks. The cold would bite the skin like a scorpion sting. The charcoals burning in the brazier had filmed over with ashes and were gradually going out. From the bedroom one could even see their faint glow.

The trouble with Begum Haseeb was that, winter or summer, she could not cover her face while sleeping. It had never occurred to her that she would have to spend a night in the icy winter of Shimla. As the charcoals died down in the fireplace Zeba turned on her side. Her sleep was disturbed. She appeared to be restless. Begum turned to look and found Zeba staring at her. Why was she awake at this time of night? Begum Haseeb looked away and closed her eyes.

She thought that Zeba had been watching her bed for a long time. But why? No doubt the night was much colder than other nights but a young girl like her should be able to stand the cold. A girl at her age could sleep even on a slab of ice. And what was more Zeba had been provided with two mattresses in place of one to keep the cold away. Her quilt was a heavy one, to which she had added an Italian blanket. She should not feel cold. Or was it that the combined weight of the quilt and the blanket was proving uncomfortable for her?

But why was she looking at her mother stealthily as if she suspected the Begum was going to elope with someone? A mother of three children, whom could she elope with? And then Begum Haseeb recalled that when her husband died, everybody said that fate had struck her a cruel blow. A long stretch of life lay before her. It had been her fate so far to give birth to children while her husband was stuck in jail. Now was the time when she could lead an easy and carefree life — a time when husband and wife really come to understand each other.

People were not far wrong in what they thought and said about Begum Haseeb. Allah had snatched away her husband precisely when he was learning to appreciate the woman in her. She had been cheated. Fate had betrayed her; it had played a trick on her, deprived her of her rights. Now life had become arid for her, a desert waste. She shivered in the winter cold.

Begum Haseeb was lost in thought when she felt that someone had got up from the cot in front of her. She looked with half-closed eyes and held her breath. Zeba had thrown off her quilt and had got out of her bed. She slipped her feet into her chappals, her eyes still fixed on her mother's face. Then she quickly tied her hair in a knot, pulled on a silk dressing-gown and went out of her room. Where was she bound for at this hour of the night? Maybe she was going to the toilet. But she should have covered herself up properly. Maybe she was in a hurry. Young girls do not always feel cold. But why had she looked at her mother so warily before leaving the room? She had done it like a thief who looks around before breaking into a house.

Alien Heart

She must have gone to the toilet. Her stomach must have been upset. That is one bad thing about all hill stations and Shimla was no exception. But why didn't the place have attached bathrooms? They charged such high rents but would not provide a basic facility like this. One had to walk down the entire length of the verandah to reach the toilet. One ran the risk of pneumonia in a Shimla winter night. How recklessly the girl had gone out, and that too in a flimsy dressing-gown. She could easily catch a chill.

Why was she taking so long to return?

Begum Haseeb waited for some time more. Then she was startled by something she remembered. The other door of the toilet opened into the adjoining flat which was occupied by an unmarried young man. After finishing his M.A. examination, he had come to Shimla for a holiday. Yes, she knew that that door was always kept bolted from inside. But it could be unlatched any time, couldn't it? The very thought staggered her.

Throwing off her quilt, Begum Haseeb came out to the verandah barefoot. The toilet door opening out into the verandah was ajar. So Zeba was not there. Then where was she? Now the Begum could hear the sound of whispering in the adjoining flat. "Zeba! Zeba! Zeba!" she called out, once, twice, a third time. In the chilly dark night of Shimla, sweat broke out on her body. Then she saw Zeba silently coming back with her head bowed like a wet cat. She had been caught red-handed!

It was past midnight. Begum Haseeb did not speak a word to her daughter. She bolted the toilet door came back to their room, and fell headlong into her bed. She felt as if she was sinking deeper and deeper into a bottomless pit.

When she woke up in the morning she found that the world outside was drenched in brilliant sunshine. She turned on her side and to her utter surprise found the servant of that young man standing by the side of her bed. He was holding an envelope in his hand. The letter in it contained just one line: "I love Zeba. Can you accept me as your son-in-law?" Begum Haseeb put the letter back into the envelope and hid it under her pillow. She lay in bed for a long time. Zeba was busy in the kitchen.

Begum Haseeb didn't know what to do. Her anger seemed to have gone. Her body seemed to be permeated with a vague happiness. She went into the bathroom and had a hot bath. She came out feeling very light, fresh and buoyant. Zeba had gone out for a walk without eating her breakfast. She didn't have the courage to face her mother. Foolish girl! It took the Begum a long time to get dressed; the process seemed to be unending. *Churidar* pyjama, open loose kurta and a shawl. She looked every inch a hill woman. She went across to the young man's flat.

When she saw him, she was thunderstruck! It was Mahmood. He was lying in bed with high fever, his body burning like an oven. The Begum looked at him and passed her hand softly over his face, his forehead, his cheeks, his neck. She did it like one who was madly in love. She lay down by his side and, taking him in her arms, kissed him. He smiled with fragrance around him. He looked so serene and calm...

"Ammi, Ammi, aren't you going to get up?" Zeba leaned over her mother to wake her up. What a strange dream and how bizarre! Begum Haseeb was drenched in sweat. Zeba sat down on the bed by her side.

Begum Haseeb looked at Zeba and then clasped her daughter's hand.

"Ammi, were you having a dream?" Zeba threw her arm lovingly around her mother.

21

Begum Haseeb lay dazed in bed for a long time, bathed in sweat. "What's the matter with you?" Zeba asked her several times, pushing back the hair which had fallen over her mother's face.

"It was a dream." Begum Haseeb smiled weakly. "Yes, it was just a dream." A tremor ran through her body.

"I'll get you a cup of tea." Zeba went to the kitchen.

Begum Haseeb could not wipe out the dream from her mind. How strange, how bizarre! She had visited Shimla many years ago before Zeba was born. From where had Mahmood appeared? Everything was so confusing. Begum Haseeb recalled that last evening Mahmood had accompanied her to the station to receive Zeba. As usual, Zeba's eyebrows had shot up on seeing him and then she ignored him altogether. The train had arrived late and after reaching home, mother and daughter had gone straight to their bedrooms to sleep. They did not talk much to each other. Otherwise Begum Haseeb would have surely pulled up her daughter for being rude to Mahmood. Whether one liked a person or not, one should not forget good manners.

Receiving the cup of tea from Zeba, she took a sip and then, holding Zeba by the arm, made her sit by her side.

"Beti, last night Mahmood had gone with me to the station. Will you tell me why you pulled a long face on seeing him?"

"Yes, I did," Zeba said dryly.

"He went forward to greet you but you took no notice of him. You just clung to me. Then you turned to the coolie. You couldn't have been more discourteous."

"You are right."

"In the car he asked why you had overstayed at Aligarh. But you didn't answer his question."

"Yes."

"And when he was leaving, you did not even thank him. He had come to fetch you in his car, as you know."

"He may have."

"Isn't all this highly impolite behaviour on your part?"

"Ammi, just tell me one thing: Who first gave you the news about the Aligarh riot?"

"Mahmood, of course. But how does that excuse you of your impoliteness."

"It was a Sunday, wasn't it?"

"You yourself said that it was a Sunday and on a Sunday one could make trunk calls at cheaper rates."

The telephone started ringing in the corridor and Zeba went out to attend to it. Begum Haseeb thought that it must be one of her girlfriends. Their talk went on and on. The Begum went to the bathroom. When she returned, Zeba was still talking on the telephone.

The caller was Rajiv from Aligarh. They kept talking till the call got disconnected. Zeba did not tell her mother who had called. Nor did her mother care to enquire.

Rajiv's words kept ringing in Zeba's ears: "Aligarh looks so empty and forlorn without you." But she had no occasion to tell her mother the most important news she had brought back from Aligarh.

Back in London, Rajiv had known her brother, Zahid. They had often met each other. Rajiv had formed the impression that her brother was carrying on with an English girl whom he had ultimately decided to marry. Although not formally married, they were already living like husband and wife. Rajiv had visited them once in their apartment. The girl was Zahid's landlady's daughter and Rajiv came away with the impression that it was Zahid's own home, so free were they with each other. It seemed he had no intention of returning to India. Nor had he any intention of settling down in Pakistan. In fact, he abhorred Pakistan. Whenever there was a public rally organised by the Indians against Pakistan, he always took the lead in it.

After lunch, when Zeba conveyed all this, Begum Haseeb was stunned. "His Abba had all his life fought against the feringis and now his son wants to marry a feringi's daughter." She could not believe her ears.

"Why should you feel so annoyed? India fought against the British. Now that our country is free, we have formed an alliance with them. Our country has become a member of the Commonwealth." Zeba gave her mother a bemused smile.

"I don't like to hear all this nonsense." The Begum was getting really worked up.

"Ammi, what's there to be angry about? If you ask me, I like the idea. I shall have a white woman, a memsaheb, for a sister-in-law."

"And she will talk all gibberish in an impeccable accent," the Begum retorted.

"No, Rajiv said that Bhaiyya was teaching her Urdu."

"Who is this Rajiv?" Zeba's mother gave her daughter a puzzled look.

"Ammi, he is Rai Saheb Ram Jawaya's son. They were your neighbours in Aligarh, if you remember."

"Oh, you mean Raju? Since when has he become Rajiv? When I knew him his nose was running all the time."

"You must see him now. A smart young man, tall, dark and handsome."

"Like Lord Krishna?" The Begum tried to make fun of her daughter, in order to discourage her.

After that there was a phone call from Aligarh every other day. Zeba would keep talking for long. The call would go on interminably.

But Zeba had posed a serious problem for her mother.

After thinking over the matter Begum Haseeb at last wrote a letter to Zahid, full of complaints and demands. Seema had already tarnished her face, she had written. Now she had to marry off Zeba. "How long can this girl remain unmarried? She has almost completed her education and is now ready for marriage. I want to be rid of my responsibility towards her. You must return to India as soon as you get this letter. You can find a good job here. And for that matter I've also to think of your marriage."

Zeba read her mother's letter and then added a postscript to it; "Bhaiyya, if you are already married, bring my Bhabhi along. But come you must – Zeba."

22

Sheikh Shabbir was in bad shape. He was still getting fits as before. After shifting to Lahore, he had been under treatment there for a long time. He also had a brief spell in the mental hospital. The doctors agreed that his condition was the result of some deep mental shock, but Sheikh Shabbir refused to open up and let them into his secrets. The doctors as much as the psychiatrists had failed in their efforts.

However, of late a change had come over him. He would say his namaz five times a day and kept fasts. He had also gone for Haj. He counted his rosary all the time and, when he was not at it, he would be holding his *lota* to do his ablution. His pyjama legs stopped short at the ankle. He had cultivated a maulvi-like beard, ending in finely trimmed hair. Though he refused to admit it, his coming to live in Pakistan had only added to his woes.

From Lahore he had shifted to Gujranwala from where he moved on to Gujrat and, after a short stay in Jhelum, he had finally settled at Rawalpindi where he had managed to get a house on rent in a *basti* near the cantonment. He did no work to earn a living. For that matter neither his age nor his health permitted him to do any work.

Soon after coming to Pakistan his daughter Noori had eloped with a young Panjabi boy. The Sheikh had to do a lot of running about to trace her and ultimately he made the best of the bad bargain by marrying her to the same young man. For quite some time the young man's vocation remained a mystery. He would be missing from home for days together. Sometimes he had no money, at other times he had a surfeit. Sheikh Shabbir was mystified.

Then he came to know that the boy was engaged in smuggling across the Indo-Pakistan border. Truckloads of silk cloth, sugar, tea, betel leaves, bananas, mangoes, spices and a large variety of liquor were brought in. One day Noori told her father that even school exercise-books were smuggled in large quantities.

"But you must also be sending out something in exchange," Sheikh Shabbir asked his daughter. His sense of self-respect was not prepared to accept the fact that Pakistan was woefully short of these things and that they had to depend on another country for their requirements, obtained in a clandestine manner.

Noori was silent. Perhaps she did not know about it.

Money comes and goes. Sheikh Shabbir was not so much concerned about where the money went. What worried him most was the young man's behaviour towards his daughter, Noori. He talked to her so insolently, abused her in filthy words and of late had even started beating her.

In those days Sheikh Shabbir was undergoing treatment at the Mental Hospital at Lahore. One day he happened to visit Noori's house and found her lying sprawled in her room. He learnt that the night before his son-in-law had got drunk and thrashed her. Then, without taking any further notice of her, he had disappeared from the house in the morning while she lay writhing in bed with pain.

The Sheikh was consoling his daughter when his son-in-law appeared on the scene. On seeing the young man, the Sheikh flared up. "How can you be so cruel," he asked. "You have been beating my daughter as if she were a sack!"

"Abbajan, it's Allah's command that a woman must be given a beating once in a while," the young man replied nonchalantly, taking a puff at his cigarette.

Sheikh Shabbir's son, Kabir, was living happily in Pakistan. As soon as he came to Pakistan, his uncle Zubair had got him a job in the PWD. The salary was nothing much to talk about but his "other" income was quite substantial. There was only one snag in an otherwise happy situation. He was married to a Panjabi girl who completely dominated him. She had produced two children for him in quick succession. But she did not allow him to have anything to do with his relatives. She dressed flamboyantly, liked heavy make-up on her face and had cut her hair. Sheikh Shabbir hated the very sight of her. What irritated him most was her manner of speaking. He could make out something from her Panjabi. But when she tried to speak in Urdu, he felt as if he was being physically assaulted. Faulty idiom, wrong pronunciation and garbled phrases used out of context. The worst of it

Alien Heart

was, she mixed Panjabi with Urdu. What really pained Sheikh Shabbir was that his own language was getting spoiled. He tried to speak Panjabi with disastrous results.

An unfamiliar language and different ways of living. Kabir's Panjabi wife tried to isolate him from his relatives. Then he was transferred to a distant station where he had to supervise the construction of a canal. Sheikh Shabbir wanted his son to live contented and raise a happy family. It was far from his thoughts to depend upon his son. Allah had been kind to him and he had more than enough to live on. His money as he knew would outlast him. Husband and wife, they were just two souls who were accustomed to living frugally. He was of course worried about his illness. When he was seized by a fit he lost all taste for food. He felt like tearing off his clothes and going into the hiding. He would keep muttering "Allah, Allah!" in his sleep. On such occasions he even failed to recognize his wife and son. He blurted out whatever came into his head. Nobody understood what he was saying:

"Kill! Kill! The goondas have cheated me of my money and then looted me in the bargain! Allah Ho! Allah Ho! They have no respect for my father, nor for my uncle. My mother's tears don't move them. Allah Ho! Allah Ho! Why don't they cut me into pieces? Blunt knives. Why don't they blow me up with a gun? Allah Ho! Allah Ho! One, two, three, four, five, six. Chuk, chuk, chuk! A virgin run over by a train at the level crossing. Oh, what a river of blood was spilled! She had to die. Allah Ho! Allah Ho! They should throw away the rosary. They should demolish the place so that there is no entry, no exit. The virgin girl, soft like a bud, tender like a sapling. Allah Ho! Allah Ho! Cut off the hands of the thief. If he fornicates, give him a hundred lashes. Don't drink, don't gamble. Allah Ho! Allah Ho! It is permitted by religion to have four wives. Two women are equal to one male and a girl is at par with six males. Allah Ho! Allah Ho!"

Sheikh Shabbir would keep talking to himself incoherently for hours together and then suddenly rush out of the house. Nobody could stop him. When the fit was over, he would return home calm and quiet. He would look as if there was nothing wrong with him.

23

At that time Zahid was having just an affair with the English girl. He had not yet married her. He came home soon to meet his mother. His girlfriend did not accompany him. And Begum Haseeb did not allow her son to go back to England. She managed to get him a good job. The state government was quite willing to accommodate Sheikh Haseeb's son. Also, of course, Zahid was a highly qualified doctor. He was appointed on the staff of the Meerut Hospital in consideration of his mother's wishes, for she wanted to have her son near her.

This arrangement took about a month to finalise. Begum Haseeb was pleased that the prodigal had returned home. Now only two things remained to be done: Zahid's and Zeba's marriages.

Zahid had been in Meerut only a short time when Begum Haseeb set about looking for a bride for him. In the meanwhile, Mahmood's parents returned empty-handed from Pakistan. They had not been able to find a suitable match for their daughter Rukhsana. A couple of boys seemed eligible but Rukhsana did not approve of them.

Then she started complaining that she was feeling bored in Pakistan. In fact, the *mullahs* in Pakistan had become very strict in enforcing purdah. Women could not stir out of their houses without a *burqa* for fear of being jeered at. Rukhsana's mother got over the problem by wearing a chaddar but Rukhsana did not feel comfortable in a burqa. She felt frightfully cramped in it. Not to talk of a burqa, she could not even keep a chunri over her head. Her mother had to remind her about this time and again.

One day Rukhsana was walking along a lane with her Pakistani cousins, her hair done in two plaits hanging over her chest. Her chunri had slipped from her head and fallen over her shoulders, with one end trailing behind her. The girls were in a gay mood, laughing and joking, when they saw a bearded maulvi suddenly appear before them. He was holding a pair of scissors in his hand. "Stop, accursed one!" he shouted as he shook Rukhsana by her shoulders. "I'm going to clip your plaits and present them to a barber. Then you will have no occasion to show them off. Rukhsana was struck dumb. Luckily for her, someone came and told the mullah that the girl was not a Pakistani, she was a foreigner. Only then did the maulvi relent. And when he learnt that she was from India, he cleared his throat and spat on the ground. " A god-forsaken country!" he cried in contempt and marched off. Rukhsana spent that night in great agitation. The next day she caught the train back to India.

Rukhsana was a charming girl. She had studied in a convent school at Mussoorie. A girl of fine taste, she was fond of dressing well. Sitting in her train compartment Rukhsana kept wondering if she could ever adapt herself to the ways of Pakistan; she just could not live there. The Pakistani films were so dull and insipid. The ones that were good were a replica of Indian films. Once an old Pakistani Urdu magazine fell into her hands. It contained a cartoon showing Nehru sitting in the classroom doing a sum on the slate, while Liaqat Ali was sitting behind him quietly copying it. In front on a blackboard was written in large letters: The Constitution. Whenever Rukhsana thought of this cartoon it brought a smile on her face.

The moment Begum Haseeb saw Rukhsana she took a liking to her. She wished she could bring her to her house as a bride before the evening was over. The Begum wondered how this girl could have escaped her notice all these days. This had happened because Rukhsana was studying in Mussoorie and lived in a hostel there, visiting her home town for a short while only after long intervals. Her father was a stooge of the British government, who had later started hob-nobbing with the Muslim League. He knew Sheikh Mujeeb, but there was no social intercourse between the two families.

Zeba knew her mother's weakness. To forestall her mother from taking a false step, she lost no time in showing her the photograph of Zahid's English girlfriend. "Ammijan, you are worrying over Zahid Bhai's marriage for nothing," she said. "He has already selected a girl for himself."

"Who's she?" Begum Haseeb gave the photograph a cursory glance and threw it away.

"One can't remove a young man's sweetheart from his heart just by throwing away her photograph," Zeba said, picking up the photograph. "Just look at her. See, how sweet she looks!"

"She has a white skin; that's all," Begum Haseeb said angrily.

"Ammijan, you must have some faith in your son's choice." Zeba again held up the photograph before her mother.

"I don't want to see it. I'm not concerned whether she is beautiful or not."

Alien Heart

"What a sharp nose she has, what a glowing face. And those dimples and eyes blue like the sky. Curly dark hair. Such girls are called brunettes."

"I know, I know. I have come across a brunette before in my life. A friend of your father's. He would keep on talking about her all the time. Then one day I gave him a bit of my mind and after that he never mentioned her name."

Zeba laughed. "This one could be her daughter or some niece. I have a hunch that a white–skinned girl is destined to come to our house. Then we shall have blue-eyed, white–complexioned children running about in our courtyard. They would be speaking English."

"Stop talking nonsense." Begum Haseeb got up and went out of the room.

She knew that Zeba was holding a brief for the English girl just to put Mahmood's sister in the shade. The Begum had liked Rukhsana immensely and felt that she would make an ideal wife for her son. She would add lustre to the family. Tall, slim and delicate, how charming she looked! Even Zahid's Abba used to be partial to beautiful girls and made no bones about it. Man is there to earn a living. He must work. But it is a woman who lends colour to life. She fills it with laughter and joy. And what a beautiful name she had — Rukhsana, Rukhsana Zahid!

"I won't allow any feringi girl to cross my threshold," Begum Haseeb mumbled to herself.

24

On a convenient Sunday soon after, Bebum Haseeb invited Mahmood and his sister to lunch. Zeba had started teaching in a school and it was her day off. Zahid was also off duty from his hospital that day. When Mahmood and Rukhsana arrived, Zeba took the latter to her room and they remained there till lunch was announced. Zahid and Mahmood were left to themselves in the drawing-room. Mahmood felt cheated. He had hoped with his sister being with him he would have an opportunity of enjoying Zeba's company.! He felt that of late she tried always to keep at a distance from him. A chat with her may help to clear the misunderstanding between them. To his chagrin, the more her mother came closer to him, the more Zeba drifted away. They had even stopped speaking with each other.

Zahid was happy to get this opportunity of having Mahmood exclusively to himself. He had realised that Mahmood's views were a bit lopsided, for all the time he felt that Islam was in danger. Specially, the future of Muslims living in India looked bleak to him. Pakistan, according to Mahmood, was their only hope. Pakistan, which had come into being on the basis of the two-nation theory, could again revive the hallowed traditions of Islam.

"Can we apply the same rules to life today that our Prophet had announced fourteen hundred years ago?" Zahid asked.

"Of course, we can," Mahmood said with the resoluteness of a fanatic.

"You mean that if someone steals, his hand should be chopped off?"

"Certainly."

"And if someone looks at another's wife?"

"Both his hands and feet should be chopped off."

"Should women live in purdah?"

"Of course, they should."

Rukhsana's image as she had got down from the car a short while ago and disappeared into the house with his sister – floated before Zahid's eyes. She was wearing a strawberry red sari, a rose tucked in her Ajanta style bun of hair. With red lips, a red bindi on her forehead and real stones dazzling in her earrings, she had flitted past him like a flame. One glance, and Zahid's eyes remained glued to her feet, their nails painted red.

"The Prophet has allowed a man to marry four wives."

"Of course, provided he can bestow equal love on all the four wives. At the same time, the Prophet has said that it was not easy for a husband to be equitably fair to all his wives. It is inherent in the situation that he would be partial to one at the cost of the others."

"So a man must make do just with one wife. All I wanted to say was that the tenets of Islam must be viewed in the correct perspective. One must go to the essence of the Prophet's teachings. The Muslims will have to keep in step with the times."

Zeba had pulled down the window curtains of her room. She and Rukhsana were dancing hand in hand to the tune of an LP disc that Zahid had brought with him from England. It was a soft melody, like a bottle of wine gently bubbling at the neck. When tired of dancing, they sprawled in bed and lit cigarettes.

After a while Rukhsana recited a poem by the Pakistani woman poet Parveen Shakir:
When the evening ripples down into the eyes
And the eyelids glow like the setting sun
Like the *kajal* rainbow languishing in them
Then look at him through the magic of my sight
And caress him with the flutter of my eyelids.

As the poem finished Zeba and Rukhsana lay still and silent for a long time. All this while Begum Haseeb was busy in the kitchen. First she supervised the cooking and then had the table laid. She was pleased that Zahid and Mahmood were sitting together in the drawing-room, smoking cigarettes and chatting.

Zeba had a sudden whim and persuaded Rukhsana to change her dress. She gave her a churidar pyjama, a *doria* kurta and floral-print *dupatta*, and helped Rukhsana to put them on. Untying Rukhsana's bun, she parted her hair in the middle and wove it into a plait. Putting on Panjabi shoes, when Rukhsana looked at herself in the mirror, she exclaimed, "Hai, Allah, I look like Heer!" Then Zeba put on a qawwali on the cassette recorder:

When my pain becomes articulate,

I discover my real identity. (Faiz)

The qawwali had just started when Begum Haseeb knocked at Zeba's door. "The food has been laid on the table," she announced.

Everybody looked at Rukhsana with surprise when she appeared in her new dress. Begum Haseeb went to her room and came back with a string of flowers which she offered to Rukhsana. Rukhsana wound it round her plait and bowed to Begum Haseeb in gratitude.

The table was laden with food. "Looks like a wedding feast!" Rukhsana exclaimed.

"Not one but two" Begum Haseeb said to herself and guided them to their seats.

The lunch was indeed lavish – tandoori chicken, baked fish, murg mussalam, biryani, seekh kabab, do piaza gosht, peas cooked with cheese, cheese saag, naan, baked tandoori parathas and a variety of desserts including shahi tukra. The Begum had herself supervised the cooking. The variety and abundance were breathtaking. They didn't know where to begin and what to eat and what to leave.

"You must have had a hand in it," Zahid asked Zeba, looking at Rukhsana's dress and make-up.

"She looks like a schoolgirl," Mahmood murmured.

"That's why I wear a sari," Rukhsana replied. "Otherwise I would have to wait till eternity before I'm considered grown-up."

"Poor girl, she has travelled all over Pakistan but nobody cared to accept her," Mahmood teased her.

"Thank God that my hair was saved. He was going to cut it off." Rukhsana was thinking of that maulvi of Rawalpindi.

Zeba narrated the story to Zahid.

"What's going to be the fate of such a country?" Zahid wondered gloomily.

"What's wrong with it?" Mahmood asked.

"Would you insist that your wife observe purdah?" Zeba asked him directly.

Mahmood did not know how to answer the question, and looked flustered.

25

Rajiv and Swarna had come to Meerut for the weekend. They were staying with a relative but they spent most of their time at Begum Haseeb's where they were feted and thoroughly enjoyed themselves. Begum Haseeb had also invited Mahmood and Rukhsana to tea that evening. Mahmood smoked but did not drink, whereas Rajiv relished liquor but did not care much for cigarettes. Zahid both drank and smoked. As for Zeba she smoked on the sly and Rukhsana smoked for the fun of it. But neither of them smoked in the presence of the menfolk. Rajiv had spent many years in England, yet he was a vegetarian, while Swarna was trying to acquire a taste for meat, that is, fish and chicken. Zahid, on the other hand, could not tolerate lean meat. He ate mutton or beef and also liked pork, of all things. Mahmood, however, had the usual aversion for pork.

They had a long session at cards. Then Mahmood started feeling despirited for he was losing consistently. He partnered every one of them by turns and still kept on losing. Only Zeba had refused to partner him. "No, Baba, I don't want to have a Pakistan here," she said.

Begum Haseeb felt happy, very happy. She used to have such gay parties in her home when her husband was alive. They used to play cards till late at night. They drank and smoked and there was special paan for the connoisseurs of this delicacy. Some liked spiced paan, others sweet paan and there were those who liked paan with tobacco. Begum Haseeb catered to all tastes. Some people who shunned meat publicly had access to it at the Sheikh's table. During the month of Ramzan many Muslims came to his house during the day for a smoke which was forbidden during the period of fasting. Even the Superintendent of Police, when he could make it, came to their house for a drink. Yet, when he received orders to arrest the Sheikh for his political activities, the S.P. would take him into custody without feeling bad about it.

They were still playing cards when Zeba switched on the radio for the news. The economy of Pakistan was in shambles. The prices of ordinary commodities were soaring. Strikes and lockouts were on the increase.

"Now is the time to start a war with India," Zahid said.

Alien Heart

"Why?" Mahmood looked at him startled.

"To divert the people's attention."

"And Ayub has been promising his people that he would grab Kashmir for them," Rajiv said. "How long can he go on making such false promises?"

"You people talk as if you are members of the Pakistan President's cabinet," Mahmood remarked sarcastically.

"They may not be, Bhaijan," Rukhsana tried to explain, "but there's such a thing as common sense."

"And only Indians have a monopoly of this common sense," said Mahmood looking down his nose. This time again he had got useless cards.

"It appears you have come from across the border." Zeba pulled Mahmood's leg.

"Only his body is in India, his heart is always somewhere across the border," Rukhsana had a fling at her brother.

"I think Mahmood has never visited Pakistan," Zahid said.

"That's the whole trouble," Rukhsana said. "If he had had a taste of it like me, he would not run down his own country like this."

"A one-eyed man is supreme among the blind." Mahmood threw down his cards. He had lost the game again.

"Unless Zeba partners you, I see no chance of your winning," Rukhsana said.

But where was Zeba? Perhaps she had gone to the kitchen. It was quite late by now. Begum Haseeb had retired to her room leaving her daughter to attend to the guests. Someone had asked for coffee. While making coffee in the kitchen, Zeba became aware that Rajiv had quietly followed her and was looking at the coffee cup from behind her back. She felt warm breath on her neck. She stepped back, somewhat confused, and she was in Rajiv's arms. She turned her head and looked into his eyes. The next moment Rajiv's lips were on her lips, like two petals of a flower caressing each other. Zeba sank into Rajiv's embrace.

Mahmood had decided that he would play the next game only in partnership with Zeba. He waited for her. After a while Rajiv came back and offered Rukhsana her cup of coffee that Zeba had made for her. Only Rukhsana was a coffee-addict; she felt like having coffee every other hour. Zeba had still not reappeared. Mahmood kept puffing at one cigarette after another while waiting for her. Others continued to play. Rukhsana was again on a winning spree.

"The wretch! Whenever she partners me, she loses and makes me lose also," Mahmood said testily, looking at his sister.

"That's the whole point, Bhaijan," Rukhsana retorted. "That's why they say that partnership between brother and sister never clicks at a game of cards."

"I'll go and find Zeba," Swarna offered. "It seems she has started preparing breakfast."

"I tell you she must be lying in bed counting the stars," Rukhsana said.

Swarna went into Zeba's room. She was indeed lying in bed but she was not counting the stars. She was crying and her pillow was wet with her tears. She almost screamed as she saw Swarna enter. She clung to Swarna crying all the more. It did not take Swarna long to get at the root of the matter. "Apa, I'm really sorry," Swarna said. "You must forgive him. You have cast a spell on him. He fell in love with you the very moment he set his eyes on you. I have been trying to make him see reason. But he would not listen. He is a disgrace to our family."

"No, no, no!" Zeba put her hand on Swarna's mouth.

26

Not many days had passed when there were rumblings of war between India and Pakistan. The movement of troops along the borders increased and there were border incidents almost every day. That evening Mahmood was sitting at Begum Haseeb's place. For some days past everybody had been avoiding him and perhaps that was one reason why the Begum was trying to be nice to him. She would send for him specially when a new problem arose between the two countries. She was curious to know Mahmood's views.

She had made a paan for Mahmood and was offering it to him when Zahid arrived. He was holding an English magazine in his hand. "Mahmood, you got annoyed that day with me," he said holding out the magazine to him. "I had told you that Pakistan would again raise the bogey of Kashmir."

"But they have already started the war," Begum Haseeb said. She looked very worried. Her family was divided between India and Pakistan. Her elder brother-in-law was lying ill in Pakistan. The younger brother-in-law was an engineer and his sister's husband was colonel in the Pakistani army. He had recently been elevated to the rank of brigadier. And there were so many other relatives. One daughter was living in Amritsar, so close to the border.

"Everyone fights for his own rights," Mahmood said. "The Pakistan government has held an election to know the people's mind."

"That they should attack India,?" Begum Haseeb gave him a surprised look.

"No, to know whether they should establish control over Kashmir," Mahmood said in a low but deliberate tone.

Zahid bit his lower lip. The telephone rang. He went to attend to the call. Mahmood began reading the magazine. He ran his eyes over a part of the text and then dumped it on the table. Perhaps he found it disagreeable because it was not in accord with his views. Begum Haseeb picked up the magazine to glance through it while Mahmood lighted a cigarette. By then Zahid returned to the room. He had decided that he would thrash the matter out with Mahmood to its logical end.

"Mahmood, you must have read in the magazine about the election you were alluding to," Zahid began. "It was a stage–managed affair. Only 20 per cent people in that country are literate. Of them three per cent are women who live in purdah. Of the remaining 17 per cent, 7 per cent have been deprived of the right to vote. This includes government servants, school and college teachers and journalists."

"So what? This is the general pattern in all backward countries." Mahmood had not found Zahid's argument convincing.

"You must have also read the allegation that the Muslim League collected fifty thousand rupees to hold a reception for General Ayub and people were taken to the Karachi airport in hired trucks."

"There's nothing unusual about it," Mahmood said. "In our country the Congress squanders lakhs of rupees on such occasions."

"You must have also read that after the election, those people in General Ayub's constituency who had voted against him were attacked by the goondas at the instance of the General's son, Guhar Ayub. These hirelings set fire to their houses and molested their women. Many people were shot, while the police stood by watching. The pity of it is that these unfortunate people belonged to a colony of refugees who had migrated to Pakistan from India in search of their salvation."

"If they had not gone over to Pakistan, they would have met the same fate here. You know what happend in Rourkela yesterday?" Mahmood resolutely stuck to his ground.

"In East Pakistan they are having hartals in so many places. Mills and factories are lying idle. The police resort to firing at the flimsiest pretext. West Pakistan appears to be sitting over the mouth of a volcano. The government has started training infiltrators and they have already gone into Kashmir."

"Tell me, what other course is open to Pakistan?" Mahmood defiantly held his brief for Pakistan.

"Mahmood, do you think India would take it lying down? Won't we give them a suitable reply?" Zahid never lost his temper. But the way Mahmood was arguing, he could not control himself.

All this while Begum Haseeb was engrossed in reading that article in the magazine. She realised that the discussion was fast becoming acrimonious and it made her feel bad. Then she saw Zeba coming. Mahmood stubbed out his cigarette and walked away. He thought he would try to have a word with her in the driveway where they would be alone. But he was disappointed. Zeba got down from the *ricksha,* paid the *rickshawala* and went towards the flowerbeds on the farther side of the lawn. Begum Haseeb was very patiently trying to explain things to Zahid when she happened to look outside. From the way Zeba had drifted towards the lawn, the Begum knew that she had deliberately done it to humiliate Mahmood. For a moment she forgot Mahmood's outlandish behaviour and her anger turned to Zeba. She spoke sharply to Zeba as she entered the room. "Was that proper? What do you mean by humiliating a guest? One should not forget one's manners."

"Ammijan, what has happened?"

You tried to avoid Mahmood and went across the lawn," the Begum said.

"And I think he got up in a hurry so that he could meet Zeba in driveway." Zahid laughed.

"Zahid, beta, this is not a laughing matter." Begum Haseeb was looking annoyed.

"Yes, Ammijan you're right." Zeba nonchalantly sat down in a chair. "I swear by Allah that I had not seen Mahmood when I crossed the lawn. But, if I had seen him I would certainly have gone across the lawn, even if I did't need to do so."

Zahid started laughing.

"But what's his fault?" Today Begum Haseeb was determined to decide the matter one way or another.

"Ammi, let's not talk about it," Zeba said. "I don't want to take the lid off." She was anxious to cut the matter short.

"It's nothing," Zahid said. "He has just lost direction. He will soon find his way back."

"Zahid bhai, you don't know, this man is a poisonous snake."

"What nonsense are you talking? Toba!" Zahid was not prepared to listen to such harsh words about Mahmood.

"I'm talking sense. I'm telling you the truth." Zeba felt that she must unburden herself. She had been carrying this secret like a heavy load on her head for too long.

"Zahid said, "The way he thinks, the way he talks, he's not alone in this. There are so many like him in India. And mind you, this malady is not confined to the Muslims alone. Even the Sikhs are raising slogans for Khalistan. And the Hindus are even two steps ahead them. 'Hindu Rashtra' – the Land of the Hindus, it's similar to the cry for Pakistan. Just yesterday China slapped us in our face and today so many Indians are prepared to follow China. They claim that Mao is their guiding star."

"Mahmood is the most dangerous of them all," Zeba's patience was getting exhausted.

"May I know why?" Begum Haseeb asked in an angry tone.

"Ammijan, you will recall that it was a Sunday when Mahmood came and told you that riots had broken out in Aligarh."

"Yes, I do recall his telling me that."

"But no riots had started in Aligarh on that day. The riots broke out the following evening."

"What do you mean?" Zahid looked at his sister startled.

"I leave it to you to draw your own conclusion."

27

That evening Zeba had gone across the lawn to see if more buds had sprouted on the black rose bush. Last time while they were strolling on the lawn, Rajiv had tucked a half-blown bud into her hair. Call it infatuation, but she was eager to know when the next bud would blossom, so that she could tuck it into her hair. The black rose had become a symbol of love between her and Rajiv. It was beautiful, delicate and fragrant like him – but also dark and foreboding.

Sitting alone these days Zeba would watch the soft rain falling in a thin spray till it became a shower as if the rain-clouds were unable to bear their heavy burden. The rain beat down submerging the land under water. The rain-washed branches of trees dripped as they swayed in the wind. The buds opened their eyes and yawned in languor. Then they squandered their smiles, catching the gaze of the passersby. A joyous impulse rippled over the land, making it turn on its side, eager to clasp everything around to its heart in exhilaration.

Then menacing clouds appeared on the horizon and a heavy storm rose like a dark mountain and seemed to move like a herd of unruly elephants on the rampage. The lightning flashed like an enraged serpent, slithering out to sting. The clouds thundered and boomed. The storm burst, followed by hail falling thick and fast in the gusty wind. Morose and despondent, Zeba would lie alone in her room, the door bolted from inside and the curtains drawn.

The more she thought of it the more bewildered she felt, as if she were trudging down a blind alley. Another step and her head would strike against a stone wall. Nobody would take any notice of her much less listen to her. Soon she would start feeling stifled as if she were descending into a blind well, the darkness getting thicker layer by layer. Her mother had not relented insofar as Seema was concerned, though much time had passed and much water flowed under the bridge. After Mahatma Gandhi's martyrdom, the Begum had got over her communal fears but she had not been able to forgive her daughter. She had not even wanted to meet her. Seema's brother and sister sometimes visited her but the Begum never evinced any interest in such meetings. How then, would she allow her other daughter to have anything to do with a Hindu boy? Zeba thought she should shut herself up on a room and not open it again.

Rajiv belonged to an orthodox Hindu family. His parents had installed a deity in their house. They did *havan* every day and put sandal paste on their foreheads and rang the temple bell. They kept fasts and devoutly

Alien Heart

observed all the rituals. Rajiv had lived in England for a number of years and yet he remained a vegetarian. He would say with winsome naivete, "Whenever I had any difficulty about food I got over it by going hungry."

After that day when he kissed Zeba, she would tease him time and again, "Rajiv, don't forget these lips are polluted by my meat-eating." Rajiv would look into her eyes and kiss her lips again.

She said, "Rajiv, say it in words." But he would not stop kissing her.

Zeba said, "Stop it, I want to tell you something". But he sealed her mouth with his lips.

Zeba said, "Rajiv, what will my mother say? I'm answerable to her for my conduct." In reply, he hugged her again, this time more tightly as if he was planting her image in his heart.

What long letters he wrote to her! Swarna would be amused. While in England he wrote letters only to ask for money. He wrote to Zeba almost every day. In addition, he telephoned her. After making the call he would sit down to write to her again. A madness seemed to have possessed him. No one could have loved a girl with such frenzy. Zeba would try to make him see the absurdity of such impetuous behaviour but got carried away by her own impulses. She felt helpless like a straw in the wind. While trying to restrain Rajiv, she would herself be swept off by her own passion.

Rajiv's family and Zeba's mother's family had known each other for generations. They conformed to the old adage that neighbours are like kith and kin. But sometimes Zeba became apprehensive. "There will be a lot of fuss, and a lot of mud thrown at us. We shall all earn a bad name. They would denigrate Abba. But most of all they will blame Ammi."

Her poor Ammi! Her poor Abba!

28

There was a time when they celebrated Holi at the Sheikh's place with great fervour. Zeba was very young at that time but she still had a faint memory of it. After Abba's death the celebrations became rather tepid. Then, after Seema's marriage, her mother had stopped having anything to do with the Hindu families of the neighbourhood. She scrupulously avoided them as far as she could. One day Zeba casually remarked, "Ammi, we haven't celebrated Holi for a long time."

"No Muslim family ever celebrates Holi", Begum Haseeb said testily.

"I know, Ammi. But strictly speaking, Holi is not exclusively a Hindu festival," Zeba said. "It's a national festival."

Since the day the Begum had observed that Zeba was getting closer to Rajiv, she had become cold towards her circle of Hindu friends.

"Who doesn't like to sing, dance and play the drum? People start singing and dancing many days ahead of the festival. They just let themselves go." Zeba sounded as if she were reading from a book. "They boil *tesu* and *dhak* flowers in huge jars so that water takes on a deeper colour. And then there are gulal and *abeer* to create a symphony of colours. Oh, it's such an enjoyable festival."

"All this is taboo in Islam." Begum Haseeb clearly disapproved.

"Ammi, during the Mughal days, they celebrated Holi with great show. The Mughal emperors themselves participated in the festivities. There was much dancing and drinking."

Begum Haseeb remained silent, as if what Zeba was saying was beneath her notice.

"Bahadur Shah Zafar also celebrated Holi. He wrote verses for the occasion :
Stop spraying coloured water on my face.
Look, Kanwarji, you're in for tongue-lashing."

Begum Haseeb pretended she was not listening to her daughter.

"During Nawab Asif-ud-daula's time, Holi was marked by great fun and gaiety."

Begum Haseeb's forehead furrowed. "For the nawabs of Lucknow, any excuse was good enough to indulge in buffoonery," she remarked.

"They staged operas in which the God Indra was shown holding court. Coloured water was sprayed, red powder flew in the air, and there was drinking and dancing and singing. The poor were fed and money given to them."

Nothing could be sillier." Begum Haseeb looked most disinterested.

"Ammi, it was not a Hindu custom to feed the poor and give them money in charity. It was introduced by Muslims. That was their contribution to the festival."

"What is there to boast of?" Begum Haseeb was not impressed.

"They just didn't stop at that. Every *faqir*, every indigent person, was given a rupee each in charity."

Begum Haseeb heard her daughter in sullen silence.

"Ammi, we are Indians. This is our heritage."

"Yes, of course," Begum said sarcastically.

"Ammi, tell me, did Abba celebrate Holi or not?"

As if someone had opened the most glorious chapter of a book, Begum Haseeb's mood suddenly changed. Her expression softened as some pleasant memories became manifest on her face.

"I still remember two happenings during Holi," she said, lapsing into a reminiscent mood. "I was not married at that time. My father and mother had come to Meerut from Aligarh to see the proposed bridegroom. Your grandfather received them with great warmth. But his son was nowhere to be seen. It was the day of Holi. They waited for a long time. They had finished eating when he suddenly appeared, his face coloured red and blue. He looked as if a demon had descended on the courtyard!

"My parents were stunned. Was this the boy whose hand they had sought in marriage for their daughter? And now that they had come to finalise the relationship, the young man turned out to be a clown. He looked so grotesque as he stood before his would-be in-laws. It was ultimately decided that they would stay over in Meerut for the night. The boy was washed, scrubbed and cleaned. It took the whole day to do the job. Many cakes of soap were finished on him. It was only then that he was considered fit to be exhibited to his in-laws."

"Ammi, you mean you had never seen Abba before your nikah?"

"Most certainly I had." The Begum's cheeks turned red. "Once the engagement was confirmed, there was no bar against our meeting."

"Your parents gave you permission?" Zeba cast a surprised look at her mother.

"It wasn't quite like that," Begum Haseeb said, looking a bit embarrassed. "But we somehow managed to meet on one pretext or another. And through some agency or another."

"And Ammi, what is the other pleasant memory of Holi that you wanted to tell me about?" Zeba wanted to keep her mother engaged in talk.

"It was another day of Holi. People were roaming all over the town, sprinkling coloured water and gulal on each other shouting "Holi hai! Holi hai!" I was alone in the house, your Abba being in the feringi prison at that time. I felt sad as I stood in the window watching the gay revellers. I felt all the lonelier for it. Suddenly I saw a party of revellers entering our *kothi* singing and dancing. And then I couldn't believe my eyes. Your Abba was leading the party! He had been released from jail without any prior intimation. He was on the way home when the revellers caught him and asked him to join them. He had come home playing Holi. Could anything be more fantastic? Nobody will believe it now."

29

And then Begum Haseeb committed a mistake — an inadvertent mistake — for which she had to suffer endlessly. One morning the mail arrived while Zeba was away and there was a letter for her. There was nothing unusual about it for there were always letters for Zahid, for Zeba and for the Begum herself. The Begum had never taken much notice of other's letters but that morning, on some strange impulse, she opened Zeba's letter to read.

It was a letter from Rajiv. The ground swayed under her as she read through the letter. She then put the letter back into the envelope and, after sealing it, left it with the others received by the morning mail.

The Begum's mind was in great turmoil as she lay in bed thinking over the letter. They had moved far closer to each other than she had imagined. She was also convinced that, though Zahid had no hand in it, he was in sympathy with them. In any case, Zahid was fully aware of his sister's infatuation for Rajiv. Begum Haseeb felt angry about the whole affair. Why must she be punished for her children's misdeeds? And she a widow at that? Why should she be crucified for their sins? The irony of it was that the Begum had put the noose round her own neck. She should not have read Zeba's letter. It was an unforgivable action, no less intractable than Zeba's own offence; for the Begum considered it to be an offence on her daughter's part to have fallen in love with Rajiv. What was worse, she could not even admit before Zeba that she had looked at her private mail.

The Begum feared that things had gone too far and if she tried to restrain Zeba, she might only end up by taking the final plunge. She would not hesitate to follow in the footsteps of Seema who had already set an example before her. The Begum's spirits drooped as she thought of the harrowing consequences. Her face would get blackened. She was so much exercised over the whole affair that she lost her appetite. She had become ill of a malady for which there seemed to be no cure. There was only one way out of her predicament. Through gentle persuasion she must dissuade Zeba from following this course. If she managed to bring Zeba round, she would take her away to Pakistan. But Pakistan was on the warpath and was every day causing fresh provocation to India. War could flare up any moment.

Begum Haseeb became a helpless witness to what was going on around her. Every day a heavy blue envelope would arrive for Zeba in the mail. And there were phone calls, sometimes from this side and sometimes from that. Begum Haseeb felt as if someone was piercing her heart with a sharp knife and then cutting it into pieces. The worst of it was when Zeba asked her why she was so downcast. "Ammi, why do you look so glum these days?" Her question would go through the Begum's heart like a bullet.

Zahid and Zeba often brought up Rajiv's name in their talk and said nice things about him. "He's so liberal-minded, an ideal Indian. Just think of it, he stayed in England for so many years and yet remained a vegetarian. A man of sterling character, indeed!"

Begum Haseeb would feel as if someone had slapped her face. She seemed to be hovering between two worlds, and belonged to neither. Meanwhile, the widow in her kept shedding tears. She thought that if her husband had been alive she would have dumped all her problems on him and washed her hands of them, leaving him to cope as best he could. His children would have acted according to his directives and not dared to swerve from the path shown by him. Feeling defeated, Begum Haseeb would send for Mahmood every second or third day and entertain him lavishly, hoping that Zeba might one day change her mind about him. For the last few days Zahid had been careful not to bring the topic of Pakistan into his conversation with Mahmood. But the moment his back was turned Zahid and Zeba would make faces at him and talk jeeringly about him.

One day Zeba asked her mother, "Ammi, is Urvashi some sort of ornament?" They were sitting together in the lawn basking in the sun.

"Yes, we also call it *dhuk-dhuki*. Women wear it under their inner garment over the chest. I myself used to wear one."

"Ammi, is it a Hindu or a Muslim ornament?"

"What do you mean? Are ornaments ever defined as Hindu or Muslim? It's an Indian ornament. That's what it is," the Begum said naively.

"Ammi, is arsi also an ornament?"

"Of course, you should know. It is a kind of signet studded with ornamental glass. Women look into it to repair their make-up."

"Ammi, do Hindus wear this ornament or the Muslims?"

"Both. It's common to both."

"But Ammi, a tika must surely be a Hindu ornament."

"What makes you say that? Tika is worn over the forehead. It is as much popular with Hindus as with Muslims. I wore it at my wedding."

"And what is ramjhol?"

"It's meant to be worn on the foot. It's made of silver."

"I'm sure it is a Hindu ornament. Its very name says so."

"Oh, no, I used to wear it on festive occasions."

"But you have not worn an ornament for several years."

"Since your Abba's death, I haven't touched any of my ornaments."

"To shun ornaments is a Hindu custom, isn't it? Hindu widows smash their bangles on the death of their husbands," said Zeba.

Begum Haseeb had seen her point now, but she feigned ignorance.

"I don't remember anything about my Abba."

"You were ten years old at the time of his death. Surely you must remember something about him."

"Ammi, I've only a hazy memory of him. That's all. He must have been very handsome in his youth. What did he look like?"

"Well... he resembled Mahmood quite a lot." The words suddenly escaped Begum Haseeb's lips. As Zeba heard this, the taste in her mouth turned sour.

30

Those days whenever an opportunity came his way, Zahid tried to probe Mahmood to understand his mind. He felt that Mahmood had the same mentality as many other Muslims of India. His thinking like theirs was a blend of reality and fantasy. Mahmood was over-sensitive. Being volatile as well, he was overcritical of things. He was also fond of stealing the limelight. One day Zahid casually mentioned about the riots at Rourkela:

"Nowadays riots have become a part of our life. Even America is not free of riots. They happen also in Great Britain. The whites and the blacks at times don't agree with each other."

"Their case is different," Mahmood said.

"In Pakistan, they have riots between Shias and Sunnis. Between the locals and the refugees. Between Panjabis and Bengalis. The Ahmediyas often become the target of the anger of other Muslims."

"That doesn't mean that we should also start killing the Muslims here. On the one hand we swear by secularism, and on the other we practise communalism."

"Every riot can't be explained away as communal . In a society like ours which is changing quickly, there can be other reasons for discord."

"But here communalism is the cause of every riot." Mahmood's mind was firmly rooted in his beliefs.

"I don't agree with you. Often it's the shadow rather than the reality which misleads us."

"Whatever the cause, it is always the minority community which suffers."

"There is bound to be discord when we move towards progress, specially when we try to force the pace of change."

Mahmood shook his head as if this fact was beyond his comprehension.

"Take the case of Rourkela," Zahid said. "From newspaper reports it is quite clear that because of the trouble in East Pakistan Hindu refugees started coming to West Bengal. They tried to stay on in Calcutta. But Calcutta was already full of refugees, so these displaced persons were put on trains and sent to Dandakaranya in Madhya Pradesh. These trains stopped on the way at Rourkela where the refugees were fed by the local people of the city. The local people naturally sympathized with the refugees who gave exaggerated description of the hardship they had to undergo in East Pakistan. Then one day a Hindu refugee who had eaten food served by a Muslim organisation had a stomach upset and vomited. This gave rise to the rumour that Muslims were distributing poisoned chapatis to the Hindu refugees. It was utterly false. But who can stop a rumour from spreading? Hindus already suspected that the local Muslims had collected firearms in their houses and that they had set up links with Pakistan through radio transmitters."

"It wasn't so, Zahid, I was myself in Rourkela at that time. On the pretext of serving food to the refugees, the RSS people were brainwashing them by spreading false rumours against Muslims."

"But what had taken you to Rourkela at that time?" Zeba, who had just come into the room asked.

Mahmood was taken aback by the question. "I had gone to meet a relative," he said quickly recovering himself.

"The RSS may have had a hand in this game. But I feel that there was something else behind these Rourkela riots."

"All this is nothing but kite–flying." Mahmood frowned in order to express his disagreement.

"But Jayaprakash Narayan can't be wrong."

"All Hindus can be wrong where Muslims are concerned." Mahmood's tone was full of venom.

'There's no point in being emotional. Such allegations generally recoil against the minority community. Even the Pakistanis have not doubted Jayaprakash Narayan's integrity."

"What does Jayaprakash Narayan say?"

"His report says that, in the first place, the Rourkela plant was in need of engineers and metallurgists. They were recruited through all-India advertisements and most of the top posts were filled by outsiders. The local candidates in Rourkela felt very sore about this. These people included the tribals and local Hindus, also the Oriya Muslims. They were left behind while Bengalis, Punjabis, Biharis, Madrasis and Keralites entrenched themselves in the plant. The second reason was that the local Muslims, who are more prosperous, were exploiting the tribals. These tribals, already victims of exploitation, were also hostile to the outsiders."

"Which could mean that the riots in Jassor acted as an immediate provocation," Zeba said.

"In fact, riots are a sign of backwardness. It is a denial of equal opportunity to all on the way to progress." That was how Zahid looked at the problem.

"What you say is nothing but academic claptrap," Mahmood said. "As you know there were riots in Calcutta soon after Jassor. Whom do you hold responsible for them?"

"It means that whenever Hindus are oppressed in Pakistan, Muslims in India will have to pay the price for that," Zeba said.

"And this situation will continue until the Kashmir issue is settled," Mahmood said. He added "That's precisely what Bhutto, the Foreign Minister of Pakistan, says. He argues that the root of trouble between India and

Pakistan is the question of Kashmir. Till that is decided, it is futile to expect peace between the two countries."

"As against that Jayaprakash Narayan says that if Hindus in India oppress Indian Muslims because Pakistani Muslims tyrannise over Hindus there, it will only prove the validity of the two-nation theory."

"Jayaprakash Narayan has remained a dreamer all his life," Mahmood said.

"In reality it is not so much a problem of Kashmir as it is of East Pakistan. West Pakistanis want all the Hindus to be driven out of East Pakistan so that the population of East Pakistan becomes less than that of West Pakistan. In this way they want to make sure of their hold over this part of their country to their own advantage," Zahid said.

"Yes, I agree with you that the Panjabi Muslims of Pakistan want to dominate the Bengali Muslims," Zeba said.

"And the Indian Muslims get crushed between these two millstones."

"The fact of the matter is that Kashmir is the real unresolved issue between India and Pakistan," Mahmood stuck to his point.

"No, far from it," Zahid tried to explain. "In reality it is a question of the identity of Indian Muslims. As long as the Muslims of India look to Pakistan as their ultimate refuge, as long as they don't have a sense of belonging to India, their troubles will never come to an end."

"The goat lost its life but the eater did not relish its meat," Mahmood jeered. "What better proof of our loyalty can we give than to say that we have not gone away to Pakistan?"

"You may not have gone over to Pakistan but you have not become an Indian at heart," Zeba said with an air of finality.

"A country where they raise slogans such as 'Hindu, Hindi, Hindustan,' a country which allows a party like

Alien Heart

the RSS, to organise itself and flourish – how can one belong to such a country?" Mahmood asked angrily.

"Therefore, the Muslims of such a country should conspire with fifth columnists!" Zeba jibed.

"Certainly, who would not fight for his rights?" Mahmood was getting angrier.

"Is that the reason why your honour had gone to Rourkela to meet your relatives?"

Zeba, it seemed, had caught Mahmood on the wrong foot. He was incensed and nearly shouted, "What do you mean?"

"What I mean is that wherever there is a riot, some people make it a point to be present there," Zeba said.

Her words hit Mahmood like gunfire. He gnashed his teeth and stamped out of the room like the proverbial yogi escaping from a burning village.

31

Zahid said to Zeba, "You shouldn't annoy Mahmood like this."

She knew that one should not be rude to a visitor. But she couldn't help it. For some time past she had started hating Mahmood; she just couldn't stand him. He, on the other hand, seemed to have cast a spell on her mother. She could not find any fault with him and even if she discerned any shortcoming, she just overlooked it.

"She's gone crazy, this girl!" Begum Haseeb said coming into the room. She had heard their talk while walking down the verandah. The way the girl had behaved was not in keeping with the culture of the family.

"This man...." Zeba broke down before she could proceed. But now her mother as well as her brother came down heavily upon her. As soon as Ammi finished, Zahid took over.

Zeba knew that Zahid was in love with Rukhsana and that the girl had also taken a liking for him. It was so evident from Zahid's behaviour. He had changed a great deal ever since she had come into his life. Her name was always on his lips.

As for Begum Haseeb, she remembered seeing Zeba's head in Mahmood's lap. Subsequently there had been some misunderstanding between them and they had become estranged from each other. Begum Haseeb had hope that as time passed, they would again come closer. Mahmood had won over the Begum. She had come to like him for she saw an image of her husband in him. What other attributes would a widow like to see in a young man? Besides, he came from a good family. It was so difficult to find eligible Muslim boys those days. They had searched all over Pakistan for a good match for Rukhsana and had returned to India disappointed. The Begum had grave apprehensions about Rajiv. After reading his letter, her mind was always in flutter. If she could find a good Muslim boy for Zeba, she would marry her off and absolve herself of this responsibility. Now that Zahid and Rukhsana had come so close to each other, could there be anything more desirable than establishing a relationship between Mahmood and Zeba? Zeba who was the youngest in the family was very temperamental. When Zahid became a son-in-law of that family, he would look after Zeba as well.

Alien Heart

"These days young men are usually angry," Zahid explained to his sister. "Specially for the Muslim youths of our country, there is an additional reason for being angry with the world."

"Yes, I know. Most people don't care about their rights," Begum Haseeb forestalled her son.

Zeba looked at her mother in surprise as if she could not trust her ears. Was this the wife of Sheikh Haseeb speaking? Zeba said, "In a democracy everybody has a chance to safeguard his interests. Everyone can fight for his rights."

"Sometimes your Abba had sharp differences with his Hindu fellow-workers."

"There's no doubt that justice is not being done to the minority community with regard to Urdu."

"I would go to the extent of saying that even in the case of jobs, full justice is not being done to Muslims." Begum Haseeb's views seemed to agree with those of Zahid.

"You are right," Zahid said. "Today in the year of grace 1965, of the 2100 IAS officers there are only 111 Muslims. Of the 270 in the Foreign Service cadre there are only 12 Muslims. And as for the Indian Police Service, there are in all 1200 officers of whom only 43 are Muslims.

"The same is true of figures relating to representation in the Lok Sabha and Vidhan Sabhas. Muslims constitute 10 per cent of the total population of the country. As against this in the Lok Sabha of 1952 there were only 3.68 per cent Muslims. In the Lok Sabha of 1957, their percentage was 4.25 and it rose to 4.6 per cent in the Lok Sabha of 1962. The position in the states' Vidhan Sabhas is also fast deteriorating. In 1952 there were 5.3 per cent Muslims, in 1957 the figure was 5.32 per cent and in 1962 it came down to 4.93 per cent."

"I wonder how I'm concerned with all these statistics," Zeba said. "Why tell me all this?"

"So that you may change your way of thinking," Zahid said. "If young men like Mahmood raise a voice of protest they have certainly some valid reason for it."

"To protest is one thing, but sedition is something quite different," Zeba said. She was still unable to forgive Mahmood.

"Young men can sometimes go astray," Zahid said in defence of Mahmood.

"And they can be brought back to the right path," the Begum added.

Unable to understand what they were driving at, Zeba got up on a huff and went away to her room. She lay still in her bed for a long time.

Sitting alone in the drawing-room with her son, the Begum got an opportunity to unburden her mind to him. She was anxious to perform Zeba's nikah at the earliest opportunity and she could not think of a better match than Mahmood.

"But nothing must be done against Zeba's wishes," Zahid said.

"Why must we care for her wishes? There was a time when she could not spend a moment without this very Mahmood," the Begum said.

"In such matters we shouldn't do anything in a hurry," Zahid said.

"Then she will do what her sister did." The Begum became impatient.

"But we can't force things down her throat."

"Mahmood's mother has dropped hints several times. Next time I'm going to say yes."

"Toba, toba! Don't ever make such a mistake," Zahid said. "These days nobody interferes in somebody else's private affairs."

Alien Heart

"You mean a mother does not have even that much right over her children?"

"A mother has all the rights except this one. The question of marriage should be left to those who have to be married."

"To tell you the truth, I don't like the girl's ways. She will bring a bad name to the family," the Begum said with some agitation.

"In my opinion you should talk it over with Rukhsana. She can bring Zeba round. They are on very friendly terms these days."

Begum Haseeb liked Zahid's suggestion. She thought that Rukhsana would not turn down her request and for that matter she had already accepted Rukhsana as her daughter-in-law in her heart. One day she would be the glory of this house. At the next opportunity when Zeba was away at school and Zahid was at the hospital, Begum Haseeb sent for Rukhsana and broached the subject of Zeba's marriage to Mahmood.

"Ammijan, what's wrong with you?" Rukhsana said as if she could not believe her ears. "Zeba and Mahmood! A bell round the camel's neck! Mahmood is my brother and I should not say anything against him. But he is not at all suitable for an enlightened girl like Zeba. He's so wayward and stupid."

"All young men are like that. They improve with time," Begum Haseeb said in a firm voice.

"Don't ever make such a mistake. Zeba and Mahmood will not be able to pull on together even for a day. They can't be partners even at a game of cards, how can they be partners in life?"

"There was a time when both of them ..." And then the mother in Begum Haseeb suddenly fell silent.

"I know everything," Rukhsana said. "But that time is long since past. It's gone for ever."

32

The meeting with Rukhsana put the idea in Begum Haseeb's head that there was a conspiracy against her. Everybody seemed to be determined that there should be no marriage between Zeba and Mahmood. Mahmood's own sister had said it in so many words. As for Begum Haseeb, she continued to find Mahmood most eligible. He belonged to an affluent family. He was the only son of his father. And, above all, Zeba would live in the same city after her marriage and her mother could meet her any time she liked. The Begum attached much importance to this prospect because her elder daughter had cut herself off by her marriage.

Begum Haseeb could see no other alternative. After that day when Zeba had almost spurned Mahmood, he had stopped coming to their house. Begum Haseeb could not think of any pretext on which she could invite him to her house. And this frustration had started telling upon her health. She lost her appetite. She would lie awake at night, turning from side to side. She would close the door of her room and bow her head in prayer or she just cried. Every evening she would visit her husband's grave and sit there weeping. She said her namaz five times a day and counted her beads, yet she saw no ray of hope anywhere.

She got weaker day by day and was soon reduced to a mere skeleton. Zahid was worried and so was Zeba. Time and again they got their mother examined medically but the doctor did not find anything wrong with her. Even then she had taken to bed. Zeba knew what the trouble with her was. Zahid too had his suspicion about the real cause of her malady. But it was a malady for which there was no ready cure. The house which once resounded with gaiety now lay in gloomy silence.

Everything else had gone except Rajiv's letters. Begum Haseeb would shudder at the sight of those large envelopes as they arrived in the post. Every other day there was a phone call from Rajiv, and they would talk on and on in low voices. God only knew what they talked about – and what they had not written in those long letters – that they had to glue themselves to the telephone so often and for so long.

The condition of Sheikh Shabbir, who was still living in Pakistan, was deteriorating. Then his relation in India heard that he had gone completely insane. He had left home and gone to live in a shrine where he kept intoning 'Allah hoo, Allah hoo' all the time. He had shaved his head and grown a long beard. Clad in a blue robe, he would go about barefoot holding a thick stick in hand. He would not go home. He could not even recognise his own people. To make matters worse, his son Kabir's wife had eloped with some other man, leaving two children behind. His mother was now looking after his children and she was anxious to find a new wife for him so that he could again set up home. It must be a girl who could take the responsibility of bringing up step-children.

A letter came from the Begum's sister-in-law. "Qudsia, if you know of an eligible girl, help me to set up Kabir's home," she had written. Yet it was generally believed that there was a dearth of eligible boys in India, hence Muslim families searched for suitable grooms in Pakistan for their daughters. On reading her sister-in-law's letter, the Begum was reminded of a remark her sister-in-law had made in passing many years ago: "Qudsia, I think Kabir and Zeba would make an ideal couple." At that time these two were still mere toddlers Qudsia had laughed off her sister-in-law's suggestion.

There was another letter from her sister-in-law just after a week. She was greatly agitated. Her husband was seriously ill and she had already spent a lot of money on his treatment with no satisfactory results. Her daughter-in-law, as she had already informed, had eloped with someone and her daughter's husband was treating the poor girl badly. The household was in much turmoil. Once they had been so prosperous, basking in the sunshine of affluence, but now they led a miserable life. Nobody cared for them. They had lost their moorings and were having a terrible time. Begum Haseeb felt sorry for her sister-in-law. What a fine woman she used to be! Always cheerful, she never talked ill of anybody. When Qudsia had come as a bride, she had gone all out to make her comfortable. Sheikh Haseeb, Qudsia's husband, wished to live independently in their Civil Lines house. Without giving the matter a second thought, Qudsia's sister-in-law had persuaded her husband to shift to their ancestral house in the city. Although they lived apart, she would phone Qudsia ten times a day. "What are you doing? What have you cooked? What are you eating? What are the children doing? Do they find the heat unbearable?" Oh, how she loved Qudsia's children! It was her idea to send Zahid to England.

The Begum now asked herself why Zeba should not marry Kabir. If Zeba was not willing to marry Mahmood, she should not have any objection to her uncle's son. What did it matter if he had married once and his wife had deserted him? How was he to be blamed for it? Zeba could take care of his children. Another woman may not be able to fill the breach so well. Thinking on these lines, the Begum decided to take this step. She was confident that she would be able to persuade Zeba to marry Kabir. And if Zeba turned down this young man too, she would have nothing to do with her daughter any more.

For some time past Zeba had been taking great care of her mother. She would sit with her on the lawn, press her head, apply oil to her hair and do everything to revive her spirits. "Ammi, you are going to get well soon," she would assure her.

One evening when they were sitting together the Begum gave Zeba her sister-in-law's letter to read. After she had finished reading it, Zeba asked, "What would you like me to do?"

"I'm under great obligation to your aunt," the Begum said. "I want to repay some of that debt. If you agree to marry Kabir ..."

She had not even completed her sentence when Zeba groaned and collapsed on the ground. It took her mother quite some time to revive her. When Zeba came to, she fell at her mother's feet, tears streaming from her eyes. "You may kill me. Give me any other punishment but don't be so cruel to me," she wailed. "Don't banish me to Pakistan." The Begum looked at her speechless.

"I'll marry Mahmood," said Zeba at last and tottered out of the room.

33

Zeba shut herself up in her room and kept crying the whole afternoon. Her box was full of Rajiv's letters. She read them again one by one and burned them in a brazier she had lit in her room. The beautiful story of her love was soon reduced to a heap of ashes. The pledge of living and dying together had come to nothing.

Now she pulled out Rajiv's photographs from her album, clutched them to her heart for a few moments then threw them into the brazier. She had received the last picture only yesterday. She held it against her lips for a long time before tossing it onto the fire. It fell to one side of the brazier which was giving out red and yellow flames. Rajiv was looking at Zeba, a smile playing across his lips. He was safe like a tender dream behind the brazier flames. Before Zeba's eyes and yet out of reach as if he had undergone the ordeal by fire, he was proving the truth of his love.

Then like one gone crazy, she began speaking to the photograph: "Rajiv, my love, this is not a brazier in my room but the sacrificial fire of our love. Your boast that you will not let our love die was only a dream. The realities of life are harsh and the shackles of society are even more difficult to break. Love is one thing but religion is something quite different and separate. I have loved you but I was born to a Muslim family. I have loved you of my own free will, but there was another destiny playing with my life from the time I was born. I have been forced to bend my knees before that power.

"We Indian boys and girls, whether Hindus or Muslims, have to suffer the curse of our own heritage. We have inherited only estrangement. We have inherited hatred. In the eyes of Muslims the Holy Quran came as direct inspiration from Allah. It is a gift bequeathed by Allah which must be preserved in all its original purity. What is written therein is the last word. In the fourteen-hundred-year long history of Islam, no change has been permitted to be made in the Quran. On the other hand, Hindus have lived with Muslims for centuries as their subjects and yet they think they get defiled by the mere touch of a Muslim. They even refuse to drink water from Muslim pitchers.

"The Sufi mystics pleaded in vain. They moved heaven and earth, yet they could not persuade the Hindus to put a spout to their *gadvis*. Mahatma Gandhi said, 'Ishwar Allah tere nam' and tried to solve this problem in his own way. He thought that the desire to be free would force them to make common cause and knit Muslims and Hindus together like the beads of a rosary. Freedom was won but the breach between Hindus and Muslims remained as wide as before. Rather it became wider with the country partitioned on a communal basis. Mahatma Gandhi still thought that he would be able to bring Hindus and Muslims together. This would have been possible if they had worked together for the progress of the country. It would have been possible if they had both dreamt the same dreams. But no such thing happened. Before the wounds inflicted by partition could be healed, Mahatma Gandhi himself was shot dead.

"Rajiv, you are aware of the fact that my Abba was an ardent follower of the Mahatma. But he was also very strict about namaz and *rozas*. That is what Gandhiji appreciated in his followers. Our need today is to keep religion above politics. But this is easier said than done. Abba succeeded in drawing a line between religion and politics but not Ammi. Although so many years have passed, she has yet not been able to forgive my sister Seema. Ammi's relations with her are still as estranged as before. By falling in love with you I have caused much anguish to Ammi. I can't torment her any more. I had thought that after living in an independent India for so many years a Muslim woman would have undergone a change. Nothing of the sort has happened. I have at last accepted defeat. I do not want you to misunderstand me in any way.

"My love, you are getting charred and will burn away. How long can you stand these flames? There is a kind of pleasure in getting burnt to ashes, to jump into the fire to get lost in its blue and yellow flames. Don't look at me like that. You think that the fire will die and the flames will get put out and you will continue to gaze at me. How can one escape from fire? Please don't make me feel guilty. I am guilty but I'm helpless. I love you and I'll always love you. But I cannot bear to see my mother in torment. Tell me how many people's love has won in the end? Here is one more defeat. One more death for love. You are burning. Don't turn your smiling face towards me. I'm already as good as dead. The story of our love is over.

"We have to wait for the day when people of this country will consider themselves – "Indians first and then only as Hindus or Muslims. When in the eyes of a Muslim every non-Muslim will not be a *kafir* and when a Hindu will not get defiled by a Muslim's shadow falling over him. I am waiting for the day when we shall be born as Indians and die as Indians. When we shall recognise the basic humanity of Islam and the essential tolerance of Hinduism."

Suddenly Zeba thought that she saw the smiling face which had been gazing at her through the flames had burst into laughter. It was like a jasmine bud suddenly blossoming into a flower. Then the flames started fading; they looked so pale and defeated. The evening shadows had lengthened and night was approaching. There was the sudden sound of a siren. It became strident and took on a shrill note.

Kalu came running and banged on her door. "Zeba Bibi, Pakistan has attacked India!" he cried. "Pakistani planes are bombing our towns. There's a black-out in the city!"

34

"My life is already a black-out." The words escaped Zeba's lips as Kalu went round turning off all the lights of the house. Soon there was dense darkness indoors and the silence of death. Begum Haseeb, Zahid and Zeba came out into the open and tried to see each other's faces.

Kalu switched on the radio. It gave news of sudden raids on the Indian Air Force bases, and people were being warned to take precautions. Being an important military station, Meerut was in real danger. When driven away from Delhi, the enemy planes would unload their bombs on Meerut.

"Delhi may be the target but the bombs will fall over Meerut," Zahid joked.

"There comes an enemy plane," Zeba cried. The air raid siren was being sounded again.

"Enemy!" the Begum felt as if a bomb had dropped on her head. Zahid escorted his mother and sister to cover under a tamarind tree. The siren kept wailing at a stretch and now they would hear anti-aircraft guns.

"The enemy is on the attack!"

"But they are meeting with tough resistance."

"We shall blow the enemy to bits."

"Begum Haseeb felt as if a volley of bullets had been fired at her chest. Her brother-in-law Zubair was an enemy. Her sister-in-law Ismet was an enemy. Ismet's husband Irfan, was an enemy, also Noori who as a small girl had played in the Begum's lap. And there were so many more of them.

"We shall dig a trench here under the tamarind tree," Zahid said. "When an air-raid is on we shall take shelter there."

Zeba was gazing at the rose-bed in front of her. It seemed black rose-buds had raised their heads and were looking at her. Zeba turned her back on them. The hooter was still blowing.

"An enemy plane has been knocked down!" Kalu cried from the roof top of the house. He had gone on the roof to watch the fun.

The sound of the hooter changed its note and stopped after a while. Now the sky was clear.

"The enemy planes must have done a lot of damage."

"We also know how to play this game. Do you think we were caught unawares? Our bombers are capable of smashing Pakistani cities to pieces."

"Tomorrow our army will be entering Lahore," Zahid gnashed his teeth.

Begum Haseeb heard him wordlessly. She was thoroughly alarmed. Ismet, Kabir and Noori all lived in Lahore.

"We shall drive back the enemy," Zeba said.

"Ismet's husband, Irfan, was now their enemy. He had been elevated to the rank of a brigadier recently. It could be that a Pakistani unit was right now attacking India under his command. He might already be planning to overrun our cities and demolish our military bases.

There was another air raid the following day. Then another the day after.

The telephone rang. It was Rajiv at the other end. Like on other days, Zeba had not rushed up to pick up the receiver. Zahid picked up the phone while Zeba kept talking to her mother. After some time Zeba felt as if her heart had started sinking. She got up and went away to her room.

Zahid and Rajiv kept talking for a long time. Zahid learnt from him that a voluntary medical unit was being raised to be sent to the front to look after the war wounded. Doctors were particularly required on the Kashmir and Punjab borders. Zahid wanted to enlist and this led Rajiv to explain things in greater detail. Some professors and students of the Aligarh Medical College were also joining.

"I'll also go," Zeba said. "I can serve in some capacity."

Begum Haseeb was amazed at the incongruity of the situation. So they would fight against their own kith and kin? Fire at one another? Kill one another? Where was the world going? Perhaps this was what Hindus called the Kaliyug. Begum Haseeb wished that the earth would burst open to receive her.

The next day the Indian army approached Lahore. While the Prime Minister was making a statement in the Lok Sabha, the news was flashed that the vanguard of the Indian army had entered Lahore. It was within sight of the Shalimar Gardens and one advance unit had already overrun Bhaghbanpura. With great difficulty the Pakistani army had been able to hold the Indian army on the outskirts of Lahore. The air base of Lahore was now within the range of Indian guns.

"Now they will destroy Lahore."

"Lahore city is being evacuated."

"If we can capture Lahore, it will break the backbone of Pakistan."

"Lahore represents the prestige of Pakistan."

"Now Pakistan will never dare challenge India."

"This time we are going to teach Pakistan a lesson."

"We shall give them such a drubbing that they will remember it all their lives."

"Our jawans smash Pakistani tanks like toys."

"It is said that the pilots of Pakistani tanks abandon their vehicles for fear of being roasted alive if their tanks catch fire. If a Muslim gets burnt, how will he rise on the Day of Judgement?"

Such talk was driving Begum Haseeb mad. The newspapers were full of the news of the enemy's setbacks. The radio was blaring propaganda against Pakistan. Begum Haseeb felt her nostrils fill with the odour of hatred.

35

Finding that the Indian army had openly attacked Lahore, Pakistan made a formal declaration of war against India. As soon as President Ayub made the declaration, many people in India were placed under arrest, Mahmood being one of them. His house was raided and he was taken away by the police. It was also said that the police party had carried out a search of his house and had unearthed a large quantity of firearms which included hand-grenades, country-made revolvers, etc. etc.

"The news is correct," Rukhsana explained to Zahid when she visited the Begum's house that afternoon. She looked spruced up as if she was directly coming from a beautician — a narrow shalwar, a kamiz going down to her knees and a georgette dupatta. The fragrance of perfume entered the drawing-room with her.

"When did the police raid your house?" Zahid was worried over Mahmood's arrest.

"Early in the morning. We were still in bed," Rukhsana replied in a matter-of-fact tone.

"Too bad, too bad," Zahid said under his breath.

"What's bad about it? Mahmood had invited trouble himself," Rukhsana said. "We warned him several times

Alien Heart

but he was too stupid to understand. Nothing would register on his mind."

"Does it mean that now he will have to remain in prison?" Zahid was surprised at Rukhsana's indifference.

"Such people feel quite at home in jail."

"But a jail is a jail."

"That's all right. We have sent him some bedding from home. We also send him meals. And he has taken a few books with him to read."

Zahid was intrigued at the manner in which Rukhsana was describing the arrangements. It had the casualness of going to the hills in summer.

"Abba says it is all to the good," Rukhsana added. "In jail he will be saved from falling in bad company." Kalu had brought tea. She poured and offered it to Zahid.

"It's so mystifying," Zahid said.

"What's the mystery about it, Zahid, my love?"

A hush fell over the room. It was for the first time that Rukhsana had addressed Zahid in this manner. For an instant he felt that flowers had suddenly blossomed around him. His eyes closed as if he was drunk. The next moment Rukhsana's lips were resting on Zahid's lips. She had been sitting by his side on the diwan. Now she had thrown her arms around him and was kissing him, her fingers running through his hair.

For some time they held each other on the diwan. Rukhsana seemed to be in a trance. When she disentangled herself from him, the tea in the cup had gone cold.

"To arrest Mahmood ..." Zahid could not keep her brother out of his thoughts.

"Zahid my love, there's nothing to worry," Rukhsana said. "Abba says that the day he wants him back, he will get him released."

"How can that be possible?"

"Everything is possible. Won't the Congress require

Muslim voters tomorrow? All the voters in our locality are in Abba's pocket."

"Mahmood has been to jail once before too."

"Yes, but Abba had a hand in that also. He thought that it would knock some sense into the boy's head. But unfortunately just the reverse happened. He got into undesirable company. All the time he harps on the Muslims of India."

"But many things that he points out are not without good sense," Zahid said.

"The main problem of the Indian Muslims is their poverty – their economic backwardness. Nothing else but that. Give them jobs, create openings for them in business and industry, and they will no more look to Pakistan. That place is 'Pakistan' only in name. I've been there. It is hollow from inside like a shell."

"So long as the Hindus keep swearing by Hinduism Muslims will not feel reassured," Zahid said. "The only way out for the country is secularism."

"The trouble is that in Islam there is no place for secularism."

"So much so that in Urdu secularism is translated as ladeeniate or unreligiousness which is absolutely wrong," Zahid laughed.

"In fact, secularism means equal respect for all religions. But the Muslims have a feeling that Islam does not permit it."

Rukhsana obviously thought on the same lines as Zahid. He was pleased that she agreed with him. She went to the kitchen and made fresh tea which they drank together.

"I came purposely at this time. I was sitting at the hairdresser's when I saw in the wall mirror Ammijan going in a rickshaw towards the bazaar. Zeba is generally at school at this time."

"Anything special?" Zahid gave Rukhsana a questioning look.

Rukhsana hesitated for a moment then the words rushed from her tongue; "I just wanted to know one thing. I hope you have not committed yourself to any girl in London".

Zahid got up, embraced Rukhsana and kissed her. A storm seemed to burst within him. They were still together when a rickshaw stopped outside the house. It was Zahid's mother. Zahid and Rukhsana sat down on the sofa. Rukhsana again poured tea into the cups.

Begum Haseeb came straight into the drawing-room. "Beti, I had been to your house," she said, seeing Rukhsana sipping tea. "I was so sorry to hear about Mahmood."

"Ammijan, what's there to feel sorry about? Some rest will do him good. Please have some tea."

Rukhsana poured out tea for the Begum. She did it with much ease as if this was her own house.

36

"Kashmir is now a part of India," Rukhsana said while drinking tea. "Even the Muslim Leaguers in India accept this fact. So do the followers of the Jamat-ul-Ulema-i-Hind. Sheikh Abdulllah may have been removed from power and taken into custody, but Mohammed Ismail, the President of the Muslim League, has not gone back on his statement."

"I fear that in trying to grab Kashmir, our neighbours may even lose their own country," Begum Haseeb said looking very concerned.

"I feel East Pakistan is soon going to slip out of their hands," Zahid said.

"If India wants she can tear off East Pakistan from West Pakistan in two days," Rukhsana agreed with him.

There was no fresh news from the battle-front. After a while Rukhsana left for her home.

She had just left when Zeba arrived in a rickshaw. Begum Haseeb was sitting in the drawing-room, rubbing her hands to express her grief over Mahmood's arrest.

"I had gone to his house to console his mother," the Begum said, looking at Zahid. "But nobody seemed to be concerned."

"Didn't you notice that Rukhsana had been to the hairdresser?" Zahid said.

"Good that he has been caught at the very start. Otherwise he may have caused a lot of mischief."

"Rukhsana says that her Abba has a hand in his arrest. He wanted to get him arrested to keep him out of further mischief."

"Ammi, don't you know that Mahmood is a fanatic?" Zeba said. She was feeling sorry for her mother who wanted to impose upon her a boy for whom she had no liking.

"They don't realise that Kashmir is the only state where the Muslims are in a majority," Begum Haseeb said. "If Kashmir ever goes to Pakistan, the Muslims here will have no place in India."

"Ammi, Mahmood is a follower of Maula Sadrudin and Masud-ul-Alvi of Jamat-e-Islami. He says that the Indian Muslims should do *jehad* and establish a Muslim state in India. They would call it *Hakumat-e-Ilahiya*. No sacrifice would be too great for it."

"Not only that. Rukhsana was telling me that he is hob-nobbing with the wrong type of people. Arson, vandalism, communal clashes – he dabbles in all such mischief."

"Begum Haseeb got up. It was time for the next news bulletin and she switched on the radio. The war was still raging. Enemy tanks were being destroyed. Indian warplanes were bombing enemy targets and numerous enemy air attacks had been repulsed.

"Enemy! Enemy! Enemy! Begum Haseeb plugged her ears with her dupatta and came out of the room. Things seemed to have reached a final stage and nearer home a number of changes had taken place. But she could not tolerate Pakistan being dubbed as an enemy country. A brother can be stupid. He can be short-sighted. He can be a bad character. But a brother cannot be an enemy. She could also not tolerate Mahmood being denigrated by others. It spoiled the taste in her mouth. She felt that there was a conspiracy against Mahmood. He was a well-meaning, decent young man, belonged to an affluent family and it was like giving a dog a bad name. He would come to her house as a bridegroom donning a *sehra*. Begum Haseeb told herself that she was firmly resolved to have him as son-in-law.

The news broadcast over, Zeba went to the kitchen. A faint sweet smell hovered in the kitchen. She looked around and saw a crumpled tissue paper lying in a corner. Zeba bent down to look. Someone had cleaned her lips with the tissue paper. It bore marks of lipstick. She recalled it was the colour of Rukhsana's lipstick. What had Rukhsana come to the kitchen for? Zeba picked up the tissue paper and smiled. It was the smell of Rukhsana's scent. Overwhelmed, she closed her eyes for a moment.

Returning to her room, she lay in bed for a long time. Rukhsana was indeed a lucky girl. And how lucky Zahid was! Lucky indeed were those whose wishes found fulfilment. Their life became sweet like a symphony. It became like a spray of rain falling on one's face while sitting on a swing going up and up. One's hair flying in the air, chunri flapping in the breeze. If Rukhsana came to live in their house, how lively it would become, full of fun and merriment. She would set her own pace and make her presence felt. But where would Zeba be at that time? What did the future hold for her? At his thought her spirits drooped and her expression turned sad as if a storm had risen in the sky, enveloping everything in darkness. Then tears started flowing from her eyes.

"A phone call from Rajiv!" Zahid called out to her. But Zeba did not get up.

After waiting for a minute or two Zahid resumed his talk with Rajiv. "I think Zeba is in the bathroom," he said explaining her absence.

Since the outbreak of the war between the two countries, Begum Haseeb would keep the transistor on all the time and listen to news bulletins round the clock. Delhi, Lahore, the BBC, they all gave different versions about the state of the war. But they were agreed on one point – the intruders into Kashmir had not met with any success. Even Pakistan had not been able to deny this. In Kashmir Hindus and Muslims had combined and thrown back the invaders.

Begum Haseeb was greatly confused. She liked to hear about the success of the Indian army. At the same time, setbacks to the Pakistani army made her unhappy. She wanted India to triumph and maul the invaders. Then she would wish that Pakistan should not lose and be humiliated. Hearing about the brave feats of the Indian army, she would feel as if she was herself fighting shoulder to shoulder with the Indian soldiers. Then she would suddenly feel afraid and wish that no bomb ever fell on Pakistani territory. India's victory, she felt, was her husband's victory. And the prospect of Pakistan's defeat made her feel as if her husband's brother Sheikh Shabbir would be vanquished. Whose victory should she wish for? And whose defeat?

37

Both Zahid and Rajiv had British medical qualifications. They moved to the front with the medical unit. After a brief orientation they were sent to the western sector.

Begum Haseeb felt utterly helpless. She could neither ask her son to go nor could she stop him from going. Her only son had gone to fight against Pakistan. Being a doctor he was not to engage in active fighting, fire a gun or throw a hand-grenade. But the enemy could mark him out with a gun or hurl a hand-grenade at him. No machine-gun ever knows whose chest it is going to shatter.

Zahid and Rajiv were assigned to the same advance base. Zahid mentioned Rajiv in every letter and Rajiv's every letter talked about Zahid. They lived together, worked together and ate together. Before they left Begum Haseeb had made them promise that either of the two would write to her everyday. Both began their letter with 'My dear Ammijan' and ended with 'Your son'. Most of the letters came from Rajiv. They were written in Urdu but interlaced with English.

One day Begum Haseeb was sitting in her room, fiddling with the radio, when the pointer stopped on a Pakistani station. It announced that Brigadier Irfan had been honoured with the highest military decoration for displaying exemplary valour in the Chhamb sector. The unit under Irfan had wiped out five enemy posts and an entire Indian regiment had laid down arms before the advancing unit of Pakistani army under Brigadier Irfan's command. Should Begum Haseeb gloat over the news? Her own country had had a setback while her sister-in-law's husband had triumphed. The Pakistanis were advancing in the Chhamb sector with a view to isolate Kashmir from India and Irfan was leading his brigade in pursuit of this objective. If he succeeded and cut off Kashmir from the rest of India, the Pakistani army would capture Srinagar and occupy the valley.

What did Begum Haseeb want? Kashmir was an integral part of India. That was what she had said so often. Her son had expressed similar views and so had her daughter. If Brigadier Irfan's troops could destroy Indian military posts, they could also attack the Indian military hospitals. They had dropped bombs even on mosques. And her son was working in one such field hospital. Rajiv was also with him. Begum Haseeb thought that if her own country were not involved, she would have sent a congratulatory telegram to Irfan on his achievement. Maybe she would have herself gone to Lahore to congratulate him personally. He was like a son to her. She had had a hand in finalising his marriage with Ismet.

Not many days had passed when what Begum Haseeb had been fearing most came true. One morning she received a telegram which said that Zahid had been wounded on the battle-front. As she read the telegram she collapsed in Zeba's arms. Totally unnerved, Zeba immediately sent for Dr. Gopal who had his clinic across the road. As Begum Haseeb revived she repeatedly asked as to where Zahid had been hurt and what was the nature and extent of his injuries. Nobody knew such details. The Begum began running a temperature and her face turned red. Zeba again telephoned Dr. Gopal who advised her to put a cold compress on her mother's forehead. But the temperature kept mounting. After some time she became delirious.

"Why don't you capture Lahore? Why have you stopped outside the city?"

Zeba sponged her forehead with cold water.

"Why don't you join the army? What are you doing sitting idle here? Don't you know that the enemy has invaded our country?"

Zeba looked on helplessly.

"Send this ring to the Prime Minister's Fund. The enemy must be taught a lesson." Begum Haseeb removed the diamond ring from her finger and handed it to her daughter.

Zeba started crying. The ring, a gift from Sheikh Haseeb was very dear to the Begum.

Rukhsana came in, gaily dressed as usual. She read the telegram and immediately telephoned Meerut Cantonment. By evening they learnt that Zahid had got a bullet injury in his right leg and there was no danger to his life. His colleague and surgeon, Rajiv, had removed the bullet from his leg. The patient could now be sent to Delhi or Meerut immediately but the surgeon wanted to keep him under his observation for a day or two.

Rukhsana had an uncle who was a senior officer in the army and she requested him to arrange Zahid's transfer to the military hospital at Meerut. Her uncle had assured her that there would be no difficulty about it. Rukhsana also took charge of Begum Haseeb and, mercifully enough, her fever started coming down under Rukhsana's care.

"I always say that, whether big or small, war is an evil and nothing could be sillier when a war is fought between neighbours, specially when the neighbours happen to be India and Pakistan, constituting one family, two bodies and one soul. My Ammi first tunes in to our radio station. After hearing about the setbacks to Pakistan, she immediately tunes in to Lahore or Karachi to listen to their version. It is a strange war. Pakistan claims they are winning, while India insists that they are scoring over Pakistan."

"And the listeners too are a strange lot, both in India and Pakistan. They want both India and Pakistan to win." Zeba gave a thin smile.

"No, no, no," the enemy must be defeated," Rukhsana exclaimed.

Begum Haseeb had dozed off.

38

After a few days Zahid was transferred to the military hospital at Delhi. It was not possible to transfer him to Meerut. He had not been wounded only in his leg, he had received many other injuries. In fact, an enemy bomb had landed very close to him, injuring him in many places. But Rajiv had looked after him day and night and saved his life. It was indeed a miracle. Zahid was plastered and bandaged all over his body. As a special case, Rajiv had also been permitted to return with Zahid.

When Begum Haseeb saw her son her heart missed a beat. He looked like a doll wrapped up in bandages. There was no part of his body which had escaped injury. But Rajiv was confident and he assured Begum Haseeb that he would soon be able to restore her son to perfect health.

"He's out of danger," he told her again and again. Zahid, bundled up in bandages, smiled to console his mother. The Begum, Zeba and Rukhsana looked at Zahid doubtfully.

After a couple of days Rukhsana had to return to Meerut. Mahmood's case had taken a serious turn against him. It appeared that he had made damaging admissions to the police. Further investigation had proved that he had had a hand in some very serious crimes and would not be let off so easily. His Abba's influence had been of no avail. As the case progressed, more incriminating facts came to light and Mahmood sank deeper into the mess. His Abba had engaged a leading lawyer to conduct the case but, from the trend of proceedings, it appeared that he would not escape punishment. Begum Haseeb was surprised. But the more his misdeeds came to light, the more triumphant Zeba felt.

Even so she maintained her distance from Rajiv. On his part, Rajiv had decided that till Zahid had fully recovered, he would do nothing to precipitate matters. Zahid was ultimately transferred to the military hospital at Meerut from where he was discharged after a few days and sent home. While in Delhi the Begum and Zeba had stayed in Rajiv's quarters. But Zeba saw to it that she was never alone with Rajiv. They stayed under the same roof, ate at the same table, but Zeba made sure that her mother should not feel embarrassed on any account.

All sorts of alarming news came in about Mahmood but Zeba did nothing to go back on her promise to her mother. Mahmood's Abba said that as soon as the excitement of the war had subsided, he would get his son released without any difficulty. Rukhsana cursed Mahmood for his recklessness.

Thanks to Rukhsana, Zahid was improving day by day. She was with him most of the time. Zahid had spent only a few days in the forward area but he was full of stories about the war with Pakistan. In the Chhamb-Jaurian sector the battle remained undecided for a long time, each scoring over the other by turns. The balance once swaying in favour of Pakistan and next time dipping in favour of India. The Indian army comprising Sikhs, Christians, Hindus and Muslims fought like one, the cries of 'Har, Har, Mahadev!' mingling with the cries of 'Allah Ho Akbar!" and 'Sat Sri Akal!'

Zahid had got injured in the Chhamb-Jaurian sector. That day Begum Haseeb was telling her son about the distinction conferred on Brigadier Irfan. Zeba and Rukhsana were also present in the room.

"It could be a bomb thrown by Ismet's husband at your son," Zahid joked.

"What do you mean?" the Begum asked after a pause.

"Yes, it could be Uncle Irfan's doing," Zahid said in mock seriousness. "How can one be sure that it was not thrown by him?"

"That was why you escaped death," Zeba laughed.

"It's nothing to laugh about," Rukhsana's face tingled. "It's time that the Muslims of India took a decision. They must decide who is their friend and who their foe."

Zeba came up with a ready answer : "The government of Pakistan is our enemy. But the people of Pakistan are our friends."

"Uncle Irfan's bomb could have killed me in the same way as it had killed so many of my comrades," Zahid said.

"There's God's curse over our generation," Begum Haseeb said rubbing her hands in dismay. She got up and went away to her room.

"True, we are like brothers and sisters. We are neighbours," Rukhsana said. "But in war, we are enemies of one another."

"When there's truce, we shall again become brothers and sisters," Zeba said sarcastically.

39

Everybody was convinced that Mahmood would be punished. But his father still believed that he would be able to save his son with his influence. Begum Haseeb always thought well of Mahmood because she had already marked him out for Zeba. On the other hand, whenever she brought up Mahmood's name, Zeba's heart would miss a beat.

Zahid was recovering fast and he had started moving about. He could walk without any strain from one room to the other. During the day he would shift to the lawn and sit in the sun. The Begum had decided that as soon as he was well enough, she would perform Rukhsana's nikah with him. She had only to make a formal request to her people for they were already waiting for such a move.

But Zeba was most unpredictable. Mahmood's people were in a quandary. Their son was still in police custody. He was still on trial and his lawyer was doing his best to extricate him from the clutches of the law. People came out with strange tales about Mahmood and these greatly depressed the Begum. She consoled herself with the thought that it was in the nature of the people to exaggerate things. The police too were used to distorting facts. Last time also they had tried to implicate Mahmood though they could find no evidence.

Zahid's and Rajiv's behaviour after their return from the front had opened new windows in the Begum's mind. Rajiv came every week to meet Zahid. They told Begum Haseeb that the slogan, "We got Pakistan with a smile. We shall grab India with a fight" was on every Pakistani child's lips.

"That was also what my brother Mahmood used to say," Rukhsana said. "According to him Mahmood Ghazni had looted Hindustan seventeen times and had ultimately succeeded in establishing Islamic rule over India. With his fifth invasion, Babur had succeeded in laying the foundation of the Mughal empire in India. Ahmed Shah Abdali made eight raids on India. Pakistan was also bound to succeed sooner or later."

"He has a diseased mind," Zahid said testily.

"These people don't realise that the India of today is very different from the India of those days," Zeba said.

"Today India belongs to the Hindus, Muslims, Sikhs and Christians alike," Zahid said. "No doubt, the people of Pakistan are our co-religionists. But they are not our countrymen. Religion has its own place in life and politics its own. Love for one's religion is one thing and devotion to one's country is quite another. The news about the infiltrators into Kashmir was first of all reported by a Muslim goatherd of Sabrot. A Muslim villager of Jaurian refused to help the infiltrators who retaliated by blowing up fifty-one villagers while they were saying their afternoon namaz in the village mosque."

Zeba reminded Zahid: "A few months before the outbreak of the war, Bhutto, the foreign minister of Pakistan, had openly declared that Pakistan had completed its preparations to capture Kashmir."

"And the scheme, according to my brother Mahmood, was something like this," said Rukhsana. "The Pakistani intruders were first to capture the Srinagar airfield and the radio station after which they would have taken over the administration of the state. It was believed that the military move would definitely succeed and the Pakistanis would celebrate the Independence Day in Srinagar, on 14th of August, 1965. If for any reason the plan miscarried they would cross the international line in the Chhamb-Jaurian sector and capture Akhnur and Jammu, then follow up this success by occupying the whole of Kashmir. If this plan proved abortive, the Pakistani army supported by Patton tanks and Sabre jets would attack Punjab. On September 7th they would capture the bridge over the Beas on Sher Shah Suri Marg. On September 10th Field Marshal Ayub would celebrate his victory in the Red Fort at Delhi."

This dialogue had made Begum Haseeb uneasy. Such a situation was beyond her imagination. It would have amounted to a complete massacre. Neighbours never fall out like this, she thought.

"As if the people here are wearing glass bangles," said Zeba angrily.

"It goes to the credit of Indian Muslims that they have supported their country with one voice," Zahid said. "There has been a proclamation from the shrine of Ajmer Sharif that if need be, every devotee of Hazrat Khwaja Gharibnawaz should offer his services to the country. The General Secretary of the Jamait-ul-Ulema-i-Hind, Maulana Ahmed Madni, has sent a telegram to the Prime Minister assuring him that the Muslims of India would not allow the nefarious and unholy designs of Pakistan to succeed. The Shahi Imam of Delhi has unreservedly offered his help to face the Pakistani onslaught."

The same evening, Maulana Mohammed Karim Ali, the President of the Haj Committee of India, made an appeal from holy Mecca to the Muslims of India that after the afternoon namaz of September 24th they should hold a thanksgiving meeting for having successfully stood the grim test and having proved their loyalty to their country in the course of the war.

An arrow seemed to pierce Begum Haseeb's heart. Had she been faithful to her country? Had she followed in the footsteps of her husband on the path of Hindu-Muslim unity? A storm began raging in her heart. She was sitting in her room lost in thought and feeling very low when she heard Rajiv's voice. Yes, it was Rajiv. For the last ten days, he had been regularly coming to meet Zahid and sometimes stayed overnight. Begum Haseeb wanted to go to the drawing-room to meet him but her legs seemed to have lost their strength. Lying in bed she felt as if she was fast sinking into a dark well.

The next day Rajiv went away by a late afternoon train. Begum Haseeb knew that he was going but she was not at home when he left. She had gone out on a visit and was held up there. Getting down from the riksha she went straight to the drawing-room. As she parted the curtain, she saw Zahid and Rukhsana... Rukhsana and Zahid. In the next instant, she pulled the curtain together, and hurried away to her room.

While passing by Zeba's room she heard a sob. Zeba was lying face down in her bed and crying. As Begum Haseeb approached her bed, a groan escaped Zeba's lips.

"What's the matter with you? Why are you crying?"

When the Begum asked her repeatedly, Zeba handed her an envelope which had been lying on her bed. It was a letter from Rajiv :

"Zeba, if that's what your mother wants, I'm prepared to embrace Islam. I love you."

Begum Haseeb turned pale.

She went back to her room and lay in her bed a long time, drenched in perspiration. She could no longer stand her daughter's agony. She did not know what was in store for Mahmood. Of late Rajiv always came as a stranger and went away as a stranger after meeting Zahid. It had been happening like this for many weeks past and it had happened likewise that day also.

Evening approached, Begum Haseeb picked up her chaddar and proceeded towards her husband's grave. Reaching there, she prostrated herself over the grave and started sobbing. Between sobs, she implored: "My husband! My master! Tell me what am I to do? Where shall I go?"